LEVEL UP

By NIKKI. K

ARE YOU ON OUR EMAIL LIST?

SIGN UP ON OUR WEBSITE

www.thecartelpublications.com

OR TEXT THE WORD:

CARTELBOOKS TO 22828

FOR PRIZES, CONTESTS, ETC.

CHECK OUT OTHER TITLES BY THE CARTEL PUBLICATIONS

SHYT LIST 1: BE CAREFUL WHO YOU CROSS
SHYT LIST 2: LOOSE CANNON
SHYT LIST 3: AND A CHILD SHALL LEAVE THEM
SHYT LIST 4: CHILDREN OF THE WRONGED
SHYT LIST 5: SMOKIN' CRAZIES THE FINALE'
PITBULLS IN A SKIRT 1
PITBULLS IN A SKIRT 2
PITBULLS IN A SKIRT 3: THE RISE OF LIL C
PITBULLS IN A SKIRT 4: KILLER KLAN
PITBULLS IN A SKIRT 5: THE FALL FROM GRACE
POISON 1
POISON 2
VICTORIA'S SECRET
HELL RAZOR HONEYS 1
HELL RAZOR HONEYS 2
BLACK AND UGLY
BLACK AND UGLY AS EVER
MISS WAYNE & THE QUEENS OF DC
A HUSTLER'S SON
A HUSTLER'S SON 2
THE FACE THAT LAUNCHED A THOUSAND BULLETS
YEAR OF THE CRACKMOM
THE UNUSUAL SUSPECTS
LA FAMILIA DIVIDED
RAUNCHY
RAUNCHY 2: MAD'S LOVE
RAUNCHY 3: JAYDEN'S PASSION
MAD MAXXX: CHILDREN OF THE CATACOMBS (EXTRA RAUNCHY)
KALI: RAUNCHY RELIVED: THE MILLER FAMILY
REVERSED
QUITA'S DAYSCARE CENTER
QUITA'S DAYSCARE CENTER 2
DEAD HEADS
DRUNK & HOT GIRLS
PRETTY KINGS
PRETTY KINGS 2: SCARLETT'S FEVER
PRETTY KINGS 3: DENIM'S BLUES
PRETTY KINGS 4: RACE'S RAGE
HERSBAND MATERIAL
UPSCALE KITTENS
WAKE & BAKE BOYS
YOUNG & DUMB
YOUNG & DUMB: VYCE'S GETBACK
TRANNY 911
TRANNY 911: DIXIE'S RISE
FIRST COMES LOVE, THEN COMES MURDER
LUXURY TAX
THE LYING KING
CRAZY KIND OF LOVE
SILENCE OF THE NINE
SILENCE OF THE NINE II: LET THERE BE BLOOD
SILENCE OF THE NINE III
PRISON THRONE
GOON

By NIKKI. K

HOETIC JUSTICE
AND THEY CALL ME GOD
THE UNGRATEFUL BASTARDS
LIPSTICK DOM
A SCHOOL OF DOLLS
SKEEZERS
SKEEZERS 2
YOU KISSED ME NOW I OWN YOU
NEFARIOUS
REDBONE 3: THE RISE OF THE FOLD
THE FOLD
CLOWN NIGGAS
THE ONE YOU SHOULDN'T TRUST
COLD AS ICE
THE WHORE THE WIND BLEW MY WAY
SHE BRINGS THE WORST KIND
THE HOUSE THAT CRACK BUILT
THE HOUSE THAT CRACK BUILT 2: RUSSO & AMINA
THE HOUSE THAT CRACK BUILT 3: REGGIE & TAMIKA
LEVEL UP
THE END. HOW TO WRITE A BESTSELLING NOVEL IN 30 DAYS
WWW.THECARTELPUBLICATIONS.COM

LEVEL UP

BY

NIKKI. K

Copyright © 2018 by The Cartel Publications. All rights reserved.
No part of this book may be reproduced in any form without permission
from the author, except by reviewer who may quote passages
to be printed in a newspaper or magazine.

PUBLISHER'S NOTE:
This book is a work of fiction. Names, characters, businesses,
Organizations, places, events and incidents are the product of the
Author's imagination or are used fictionally. Any resemblance of
Actual persons, living or dead, events, or locales are entirely coincidental.
Based off the novel, *Wake & Bake Boys.*

Library of Congress Control Number: 2018930664

ISBN 10: 1948373092

ISBN 13: 978-1948373098

Cover Design: Bookslutgirl.com

www.thecartelpublications.com
First Edition
Printed in the United States of America

What's Up Fam,

Happy New Year! (Singing, "It's our anniversary..."). We been in this now TEN YEARS! We are so happy and truly blessed to still be able to connect with our readers by dropping new books! When I think of all the publishers, authors and bookstores that were in the game when we started that are no longer in the business, I am very grateful for the love and support of our LOYAL readers. Ya'll mean the world to us!

Thank you!!!

Now...LEVEL UP! This one is for all our LGBTQ readers and readers who just love a good story, no matter what. All I can say about this one is strap on, (no pun intended) because this book will take you on a bumpy roller coaster ride of drama and emotion! Prepare yourself!

With that being said, keeping in line with tradition, we want to give respect to a vet or trailblazer paving the way. In this novel, we would like to recognize:

Gabrielle Union

Gabrielle Monique Union-Wade is an American actress who has been in some of the most classic films of our generation. One of my all time favorites with her is, "Two Can Play At That Game." She and Vivica Fox killed that one! Mrs. Union-Wade has recently penned the novel, "We're Going To Need More Wine: Stories That Are Funny Complicated and True." It is a collection of thought provoking essays about personal true stories of power, color, gender, feminism and fame. So make sure you check it out!

Aight, get to it. I'll catch you in the next book.

Be Easy!

Charisse "C. Wash" Washington
Vice President
The Cartel Publications
www.thecartelpublications.com
www.facebook.com/publishercwash
Instagram: publishercwash
www.twitter.com/cartelbooks
www.facebook.com/cartelpublications
Follow us on Instagram: Cartelpublications
#CartelPublications
#CartelUrbanCinema
#UrbanFiction
#PrayForCeCe
#GabrielleUnion

CARTEL URBAN CINEMA'S WEB SERIES

**BMORE CHICKS
@ Pink Crystal Inn**

NOW AVAILABLE:

Via

YOUTUBE
And
DVD
(Season 2 Coming Spring 2018)

www.youtube.com/user/tstyles74
www.cartelurbancinema.com
www.thecartelpublications.com

The plan was simple.

Do one more job and then we'd go our separate ways. Life would be simple and me, a hood bitch from Atlanta, would get to run away with the girl of my dreams.

So why am I covered in blood? Why am I surrounded by money I ain't gonna ever get a chance to spend? And why is my sister, the one who I would give my life for responsible for all this shit?

I guess we all got a story, huh? You ain't lived a good life unless somebody can look at you and say one of two things. That bitch lived hard and will never be forgotten or I ain't trying to turn out like her.

For me, I guess, they gonna say both.

CHAPTER ONE
TASHA 'DOM'

POST OFFICE

Ericka got the prettiest titties I've ever wanted to lick. Not too big, not tiny, just right. The way she pressing 'em on this counter, while she fills out the paperwork to stop her mail temporarily, makes 'em look edible. She's goin' out of town for a week and doesn't want to get loaded with junk mail.

"What you looking at, Tasha?" She asked moving her hair to the side so I could get a better view. The sparkle from her Rolex watch slapping me in the face. Luckily the post office was empty because we would definitely be getting unwanted stares. "Don't eye 'em if you not gonna get with me. You know all you have to do is say the word."

I chuckled and scratched my short curly hair. "You goin' hard ain't you?" I paused. "All out in the open and shit."

"No harder than normal." She shrugged. "I figure if I keep trying then maybe…you'd come get this pussy."

"She might not be with it, but I am," my sister, Crystal, said eying her like she was the last meal. Although she was gay too, she didn't look like the type to move so hard. Her body and face said she was the girl of a trap nigga's dreams, but her attitude was that of a dude.

My sister worked with me in the post office. Why? Because for whatever reason we did everything together. It was also the longest job we ever had or wanted to have. And since the post office was new because it's in a new housing development in Atlanta, customers hardly ever came. That'll change when they sell more units. This works especially considering we have another hustle that keeps paper in our pockets.

The development, Porter Estates, had homes worth five hundred thousand dollars or more, which meant they brought people with money. And considering my sister and me lived in Adamsville, a hood in Atlanta, which was far removed from this place, we felt like we were in a different world. And yet here we were.

"Sorry, Crystal, you cute and all, but I don't do fems." She winked and eyed my sister's curves. "But you are a bad bitch though." She licked her lips. "Ain't no denying that."

Crystal winked. "Tell me something I don't know already," Crystal switched away in her blue uniform pants that I told her were too tight because they showed off her ass.

When Ericka's done filling out the form, she slid it over and touched the top of my hand. "You gonna be mine, Tasha. Trust me. I'm willing to play this game as long as you but it's getting a bit old already. Let's get together and make this thing official."

"All I can say is we'll see." I said while entering the information in the computer to pause her mail. "So when you leaving?"

She looked at the watch again. "I'm goin' to the airport now," she touched my hand again while I was

By NIKKI. K

typing. "But I know what would make my trip nicer, if you packed a bag and came with." She leaned over the counter again to show me her cleavage. As if I didn't get a good look the first time. "You wouldn't have to pay for shit, Tasha. I promise."

"I wish I could." I lied. "But I got something to do later. Who knows what the future holds though."

She frowned. "Let me guess, it's because of your little girlfriend Nikki." She rolled her eyes and stood up straight, crossing her arms over her chest. "I wish you dump that child and get with a real bitch. She can't be licking you right." She ran her hand through my short curly hair. "Because you still look so uptight."

"Nikki does me just fine in the bedroom, Ericka." I paused, not feeling like this conversation again. "And anything I do decide to do on the side with you, won't concern her so stop saying her name."

She frowned like I did something wrong to her. "Why you so serious about her then? You in love ain't you?"

I eyed her seriously. "Didn't I say that's my business? One of the reasons I could never fuck with you is 'cause you don't listen. You may have that house in Porter Estates but that don't make you better."

See that's the shit I hate 'bout these females out here. Instead of enjoying whatever we got goin' on they like to bring my bitch's name up. I don't care how bad a bitch is they will never make me leave Nikki.

It's like this. I fuck these broads out here for a purpose. To see what they can give to me. Unlike my sister who even though she got a girlfriend too likes bumping pussies so much her clit rubbing off. For Crystal all you had to do is have a pretty face, be Fem or Dom and she's jumping in. It ain't the same for me. I'm serious about my relationship.

Plus it's nothing out here for real. While Ericka is a cutie on the outside, Nikki's GOALS all around. She's sexy, smart, and proved she was down for me in more ways than I can count. If I ever do settle down and marry a bitch, which I can't see right now, she gonna be the one.

"One of these days I'm gonna get at that pussy and you gonna fall in love." She exhaled deeply. "I'm single anyway so I don't have nothing but time. Mark my words."

"Maybe I'll take you up on that offer if you watch that mouth," I winked. "Maybe."

"Yeah, whatever." She rolled her eyes and walked out the post office.

After she left I looked at the clock and locked the door. We're not supposed to shut down so early but most of the customers haven't moved into their homes yet and our boss didn't mind us leaving a few minutes early. Well, at least that's what we think. He never really said anything either which way.

While I was closing my register my sister came out the mailroom with her hair flowing down her back. She was also wearing black jeans and a black hoodie. Although we got the same father, she's shorter with long black hair and I'm six feet with curly black hair. Since I'm tall and lanky like a basketball player I knew

I was supposed to be with women but Crystal could have any man she wanted, except she didn't want none of them.

People were always amazed when they found out that both of our parents' daughters were gay. From what I hear the chances of it happening are slim but it's still our story. It made shit worse when Crystal came out before me even though I looked more like a lesbian than her. Still, its our lives and after some time people got used to it. Well, some people. My mother who was crazy as fuck seemed to be okay with it but my father left shortly after I came out. And I always wondered if it was because he was embarrassed of us.

As I closed down for the night I realized something else was on my mind. My sister always thought we would grow old together, which is why she did females wrong out in the streets, but I was tired of the life we were living. And there was something else I wanted to rap to her about later too.

I was tired of living in Adamsville and I was thinking about leaving the house that we still lived in with our mother to move out of state, maybe even to

Houston. This was gonna send Crystal off the rails because she said one thing to me every chance she got. "As long as I got you, fuck these other bitches out here."

But that wasn't enough for me. I wanted away from my crazy mother and the crime we did on the side. For real what I really desired was a life. When I was done with everything for the night Crystal walked up to me with a sly smile on her face. She looked at the door and back at me. "You ready to rob that bitch Ericka?" She asked, standing next to me.

I shrugged. "Fuck we waiting on?"

CRYSTAL

I was behind Tasha as she picked the lock to Ericka's back door. I was carrying a black plastic trash bag and we were both wearing latex gloves. Even though it was dangerous there was something that came over me whenever we hit a house that made my pussy juice up. I got a rush every time we broke a lock and finding things worth money made it better. Once we were inside I was surprised at how nasty Ericka lived. This house couldn't be more than six months old and it was already gross. There were dishes on the stove caked up with food and it smelled. She had a nerve trying to come on to my sister.

"I knew something was up with that broad," I told Tasha as I squinted my nose. "It's a good thing you ain't put your face on that trick. She can't even keep a clean house."

"Look, Crystal, just hurry up," Tasha whispered. "We don't know who saw us coming in here."

I rolled my eyes and walked toward the back. Careful not to bump into anything or do too much. Even though her place was so fucked up she probably wouldn't know anyway. "Wow, she got empty soda bottles in the hallway too," I said softly. "Gross."

"We already confirmed she's a mess but let's go to the bedroom first," Tasha continued. Once we were there she was on her regular bossy shit. Telling me to do this and to do that. I decided not to do anything until she calmed down. "Fuck you looking crazy for?" She asked scratching her short curly hair. "Check under the bed, and make yourself useful, Crystal." She turned around and started pulling open drawers.

"Why you get to check the easy shit?" I paused. "Like the drawers and stuff like that?"

She sighed. "Because she had on a pair of Christians at the Post Office. If she got more in here I know we can sell them for a couple hundred easy. Is that a good enough answer? Now stop asking dumb ass questions and move. Somebody could be coming at any moment."

"How come you always talk to me like I'm a kid?" I continued. "It's been years and you still don't respect me."

She turned to me and her eyes widened. "Not this shit again, Crystal," she sighed. "I mean you can't be serious. We on a job right now."

"You know what, fuck this shit." I sat on the edge of the bed, grabbed the remote and turned the TV on. "If you wanna see if the bitch got shoes with labels you look for 'em yourself."

She covered her mouth. "So you seriously watching TV in this girl's house like you live up in here? Leaving evidence and everything?" She paused. "Why you gotta do this each time we do a job? It's getting old now for real."

I ignored her and scanned through the channels and even wiped a strand of my long hair behind my ear. "All I'm saying is this, I'm not doing shit until you respect me and talk to me like you got some sense."

"You know what, I'll look under the bed and you bag 'em." Tasha dropped to her knees and looked under the bed. Before I knew it a black and gold shoe came flying in my direction. I ducked before it slapped me in the head. "Put them in the trash bag and stop fucking around before I break your jaw in here."

I got up and tossed the shoes into the trash bag. Please believe me when I say it's not that I'm scared of my sister; I just don't feel like being up in here fighting. Plus I got a lot of shit on my mind that I want to tell her about, but I'm not sure how she will handle it.

I met this girl name Phoenix up at the mall last month when I rolled with Tasha to meet this chick Carmen that she fucked on the side. Carmen had a job there where they sold costume jewelry in the mall for small money. It was stupid but I couldn't knock her hustle. Anyway, the only thing I was interested in when we got to the mall was her best friend Phoenix, who had an ass soft enough to sleep on and who smelled like peaches.

One thing led to another and to make a long story short, before I knew it I was breaking this girl's back out in the backseat of our 1976 red Cadillac Coupe Deville, the only thing our father left me and my sister when he took off.

Anyway, the thing was I rubbed my pussy on her raw and now I had some strange bumpy shit around my clit that wouldn't go away. And every time I showered it made me want to find that slut and choke her out because I'm pretty sure she burned me. I got a doctor's appointment tomorrow to take care of it even though I was afraid to find out what the problem really was.

Still going through the house, Tasha and me separated. I was in the bathroom when she called me. "Aye, Crystal, look at this shit, she got five hundred dollars in her panty drawer!"

I ran out the room and into the bedroom, snatching the cash out her hand. "I love when they leave money in the house." I said taking my half before handing her the rest. "Makes the job worth it."

"We good now," Tasha tucked hers in her pocket. "Grab the bag and let's go."

"Wait, I wonder what else she got in that drawer," I continued. "Let me check real quick." When I looked in one of the other drawers I saw a white iPhone. Pulling it out I said, "What about this, can't we sell this too?"

"Naw, we not fucking with no phones, Crystal." She paused. "We not selling them because they got serial numbers on 'em! If they investigate this and somebody activates the phone whoever we sold it to won't have no problem snitching to avoid robbery charges. Now bag that jewelry up and let's go!"

CRYSTAL

After the robbery we sold everything we had to a nigga who wanted to fuck me even though I kept telling him I only did girls. In the end with the $250.00 and the things we sold for money we walked away with about $750 a piece in profit. That's a good night but we've done better.

Sitting in my car in front of the playground getting high there are so many smoke clouds I can barely see my sister's face. Feeling good, I decided to tell her about my little problem between my legs. "I wanna rap to you about something serious but I don't want you judging me either. It's just that I never dealt with no shit like this before."

She looked over at me, shook her head and laughed. "Crystal, you acting like we not sisters. What's up?"

I exhaled, passed her the blunt and said, "It's like this…I—"

I heard a small buzzing noise that interrupted me. "Hold on, Crystal, my phone goin' off." Tasha takes it out of her pocket and looks at the screen. "It's Nikki, let me see what she wants. Hold that thought though." She walked out of the car but stayed next to it and took the call, scratching her curly hair.

I can't fucking stand that bitch Nikki! Since the moment Tasha met her in 9th grade she been on her and ain't been nothing but trouble for our relationship. If we go out to eat, Nikki gotta go with us. If we go bowling, she gotta bowl too. If Tasha gotta go to the bathroom she gotta wipe between her legs. I mean this bitch is worrisome and I want her off planet earth. There hasn't been a day that goes by that I don't think how better my life would be if Nikki Scott wasn't in the picture.

While Tasha talked to her on the phone, I fire dup another blunt. I tried not to listen to her phone call but Nikki just burned me the wrong way and I can't help it.

"Naw, I'll be home when I can, babes," Tasha said into the phone while smiling. She sat back in the car with the door open, her back to me, her feet on the ground.

Nikki acts like she lives with us or something. Or she's her wife. What's up with that shit?

"You know I just got off work, Nik." Tasha paused. "Just kicking it with my sister." She paused again and looked back at me. "I just said I don't know what time I'll be home now stop with all these questions."

She reached for the blunt but I didn't hand it to her. I ain't sponsoring her dumb ass conversations; with a sack I bought myself. Fuck that shit. When she stole me in my arm real hard, I handed it over to her anyway.

"Aight, Nikki, I gotta go." She paused. "You know I do and I'ma get at that pussy when I see you." She got in and closed the door before ending the call. "Now why you acting like a bitch?" Tasha asked me. "My girl know you don't like her."

"Fuck that—" Suddenly a baseball bat crashes into the driver side window. Causing glass to fly everywhere and when I looked at the person with the silver bat I saw my girlfriend.

CHAPTER TWO

TASHA

There was glass everywhere and I was sitting on the hood of our car. Why Crystal fucked with that dumb hood bitch was beyond me. Thinking that my sister was cheating, she actually crashed our driver's side window over some whore she supposedly fucked. I was about to choke her out myself since she was a Dom but Crystal begged me to mind my own business.

Tiffani, who we called Tiff for short, stood in front of my sister with her sweaty dreadlocks hanging down her back. She was wearing a red sports bra, no shirt and baggy blue jeans. She was the type of Dom who believed that whenever she wore a sports bra with no shirt that officially made her a nigga. Well it didn't.

"Why the fuck you calling my friend Mercy on the phone, Crystal?" Tiffani said to her as she glared. "What the fuck is up with you playing yourself like a whore?"

"You sound stupid as shit, right now," Crystal yelled. "I can't even lie. I'm sick of all this drama." Both of them move out of the way of a speeding car, before goin' back into the middle of the street as if it were a ring.

"It ain't stupid, Crystal. You know how embarrassing it is to have your friend call and tell you your girlfriend trying to fuck?" She paused. "Huh? You moving wrong and you don't even care."

Crystal wiped her hands down her face. When she placed her hand on her hip a dude in an Escalade honked because my sister's ass was fat in her jeans, which is why the moment we left the post office she slipped out of her uniform and put them on.

"Fuck outta here, nigga!" Tiff yelled at the truck, which was long gone. "She ain't into you. So keep it moving."

Crystal put her hand on her arm, I guess trying to bring her back to the moment. "Tiff, I can't believe you out here in the middle of the street trying to fight me about Mercy whore ass. And then you had the nerve to break our car window. Don't you realize I had to hold my sister off you?"

I nodded so she'd know it was real. Even at the moment I was willing to fuck her up if Crystal gave the word.

"You know what, fuck that car! I don't give a fuck about it or you!"

"Then what you out here crying about? Just let me go on about my life while you do you." Crystal threw her hands up in the air.

Tiffani stood on guard like a man, raised her hand and swung in her direction. She caught Crystal with a firm blow to the mouth, which she followed up with a punch to her chin. Before I could get involved Crystal grabbed one of her arms and tossed her to the ground as she kicked her repeatedly. Her head slammed against the curb and she rubbed the back of her dreads.

"Aight, aight!" Tiffani yelled.

I was about to kick her when Crystal stopped me. "I got her," she said out of breath. "Stay out of it!"

"I'm gonna kill you now," Tiffani promises hopping up. "I'm gonna beat your ass so bad like I—"

"Nigga, you ain't gonna do nothing," I said when she got up. "Or I'ma finish what she started." I looked at both of them. "What's wrong with you bitches?"

Crystal ain't the most faithful chick in the world, she ain't even nice, but I know she has a soft spot for Tiffani and her Yorkie, which she called Lil Kevin.

Out of breath, Tiffani stood up and leaned against the side of our car. Pulling my sister closer she slobbed her down in the middle of the street as she grabbed her thick ass cheeks. These bitches kill me. They were just fighting a minute ago.

"I don't care if ya'll back together now or not, Tiff, you gonna pay for our window," I pointed at her. "I'm not playing with you."

"I got you, Tash." She winked. "I just had to secure my girl that's all." She paused. "Plus I just gave Crystal two hundred dollars to get the window fixed. If it cost more just let me know." She looked at her. "She ain't tell you?"

I looked at my sister. "Nah. She ain't tell me shit."

Tiffani shrugged. "And just so you know, I went off because Crystal gonna make me kill one of these bitches out here. At first I thought Mercy was lying when she said Crystal hit her but—"

"She was lying," my sister said interrupting her. "I'm not trying to fuck that girl. She not even my type."

"Then what you call her about?" Tiffani frowned.

"Like I said, wasn't nobody fucking that bitch. I was calling that girl to see if you were at her house I think. I can't remember. Ain't nobody thinking 'bout that fat slut."

"Then how come whenever you drunk you be asking me for a three way with her?" Tiffani paused.

"Talking about you wanna rub your pussy on her titties and shit. If she fat what's up with that?"

"I asked 'cause I really wanted to see if you loved me enough to do whatever I want." Crystal said kissing her lips. "I guess I was wrong which is fucked up because I'd do it for you."

"You whores are crazy." I said. "But look, you got some smoke, Tiff?"

"I thought you stopped getting high," Tiff said throwing her dreads over the side of her shoulder so that Crystal could stand in front of her and lean her back against her chest while looking at me. "You smoking again?"

"Nah, not really." I cleared my throat. "I got something I gotta tell Crystal about later I'ma need it for." I said.

"Why you keep saying that?" Crystal asked. "You starting to worry me."

"You'll find out later."

"Oh, there go A.L.," Tiffani said. "I know she holding something."

When we looked up the street Tiffani flagged down Asian Lucy, a Chinese chick with a switch so hard it looked like her ass was gonna fall off. She thick to be Asian but I figured she got some work done. If I was single I'd still fuck her though. When A.L. made it to us she hugged my sister and then me. "What up, Tiff?" Asian Lucy asked. "What you need?"

"It ain't for me this time," Tiffani responded rolling her eyes. "Tasha seeking." There was some animosity in her voice.

The streets have it on record that one time Tiffani was crushing on Asian Lucy. But when Asian Lucy saw her at a club and they left together, A.L. was about to go down on her, she told the city that Tiffani's pussy stunk. I asked Crystal if it were true and she said nah. But she be on so much pussy that she might not know what's good and what ain't.

"What you need?" Asian Lucy asked me.

"Whatever you got tonight?" I reached in my pocket and pulled out some money.

"Shit...I got a bake sale goin' on now." She said dipping into her purse. "I got Ganja, Bart, Gold and —"

"Just give me whatever's cheapest," I said cutting her off. "I don't smoke that much to be into the heavy shit anyway."

Asian Lucy put back the other stuff she pulled out and reached into her pocket to fill my order. She was about to walk away when my sister said, "We got some Christian Lou's size six in the trunk." She paused. "You want 'em?"

Asian Lucy looked at her high heels. "Too much for me. I keep my shoe game cute but cheap."

"Well let me talk to you about something else." Crystal walked over to her and the two went out of earshot from Tiffani and me.

When I saw Tiffani getting burnt up I looked over at her. "Be easy. The last thing we need is a bunch of drama."

Tiffani glared. "I'm cool."

Crystal said a few more things to A.L. and Asian Lucy switched away, fat ass and all. I wondered what that was about. When my phone buzzed again I looked down at it. It was a text from my girlfriend Nikki. Fuck! I forgot she was supposed to be coming over.

NIKKI'S TEXT MESSAGE
U need 2 come home. I've been waiting at your house. Stop fucking around Tasha. It's serious!

TASHA

Because Nikki was mad at me for meeting her at my house late, as usual, I was on my knees with my tongue running across her slippery clit. Nikki loved her pussy eaten so much she whines when I don't do it at least once every other day. She a freak but I love it.

"Mmmmm...just like that, Tasha." Nikki moaned. "Make it wetter than ever, baby." I put extra spit on it the way she liked. "Wetter, bitch! Stop fucking around down there before I fuck you up," She continued to wind her hips in my face. "Eat that shit."

My clit was throbbing so much because of how she's talking to me that I can barely wait to feel her. She acted like a maniac when I be on this thing, which is part of the reason I love fucking her. Outside of being smart and sexier than any bitch I'd ever come in contact with, Nikki's gonna tell you what's on her mind. She knows who she is and she definitely knows how she likes to feel in the bedroom and out.

My fingers press into her chocolate thighs as I put everything but my head in her pussy. She was tugging at my curly hair and talking shit at the same time each moment my tongue flipped that button. I'm holding my breath as if I'm under water and I'm good at it too because this is our life on a regular.

"Yeah, umm, just like that, eat that pussy you sexy red dyke." She paused. "Lick it really, really good. Mmmmmm. Mmmmmmm. Yeah…you…you better not stop, you hear me? I'ma fuck your life up if you stop, Tasha…oh yeah…just like that…kill it with the extra swirl, baby. Kill it with the extra, bitch! Just like that."

I have no idea what *kill it with the extra swirl* was, or where it came from, but I do know the last time I stopped licking her box when she said that, she got mad at me for a week. She definitely could hold a grudge.

When I can tell she's getting oilier, I start flicking my tongue over her clit faster until she's grabbing my hair so rough I open my eyes and look for the Tylenol that's on the table across from us. I'm definitely gonna need it when she's done. When her thighs tightened and her legs stretched out and then she screamed out my name, I know I've done my job.

"Oh…Tasha, I fucking love you so much, Tasha…I'm…I'm cumming…I'm cumming. Yes, yes, baby, yes!"

When she stopped trembling I tear my face from between her thick legs, lick my lips and said, "You better now?"

"I can't be sure, but I think that was the best you've ever done it." She had a big smile on her face.

"You say that every time." I pushed her so that her back was flat on the bed and I pulled my pants down. "Now its time for me to get that back. Fuck your weak ass compliments."

I stroke my clit a few times and slide onto her soaked pussy. Our clits are vibrating together which is my favorite part after eating her out. The pussy be so hot and so slick not bumping would be a waste of my work. It would be something like barbequing a steak and not eating that bitch.

I gripped her ass cheeks and pressed down into her roughly. As I slid on her I looked down at her pretty face. She moaned as if she could cum again and that ain't doing nothing but making me hornier. Nikki has the complexion of a chocolate bar, real dark and real pretty. Her nose was tiny and matched her face perfectly. There's nothing about her that I don't love.

My breasts pressed against her small titties and she bit down on her pink lips. Although everything else on her is tiny that doesn't mean she ain't got an ass. It's so fat that a week back I bet her I could put an orange on that joint and it wouldn't roll off. I won a hundred bucks that night.

"I'm about to cum, Nikki, keep moving," I told her. "Just, just don't stop." When I feel my body heating up I pressed harder and cum all over her slick pussy. Her cream mixed with mine. "Damn that shit was perfect," I said. "Why your shit be so...man...don't even answer."

"Because we been fucking since we were ten." She giggled. "We pros at this shit now I guess."

"Listen at you" — I laughed — "Always talking shit." I eased off of her and laid next to her on my bed. "Now when you gonna tell me what's up? You called like a lot was on your mind so what's wrong?" I stroked her long hair.

"Why it gotta be bad, Tash?"

"I'm not saying that but I know something's up." I paused. "Now what is it?"

She looked into my eyes. "Well, I gotta tell you something. I'm leaving Atlanta, with or without you, baby."

My heart thumped and I sat up on the bed. I grabbed a fist full of my white blanket and covered myself. "You not making sense. Fuck you talking about you leaving Atlanta?"

"I think I am." She responded. "And to answer your question I never been more serious in all of my life."

I turned away from her. "So…uh…where you goin'?"

She looked down and for a second I felt like hurting her. Maybe even punching her in the face I was so mad. The last thing I needed was my mind being fucked with right now. Besides, I had plans to ask her to leave with me after I told my sister but now she sounded like she was going her own way.

She hopped out of bed and jogged toward her pink book bag on the floor. Her ass bounced as she dug around inside and I wanted to lick that clit and start all over again, until I remembered she was about to break my heart. It took a minute but eventually she grabbed two pieces of paper and walked back to me.

"Read it," she said trying to hand me one of the papers. "It'll answer everything you want to know."

I looked down at them. "What is it?"

"Tasha, please just look at them."

I took it and read over everything quickly. Before long I understood perfectly what was goin' on. She was pregnant. My eyes widened. "So, so it worked?" My jaw dropped.

"Yes, baby," she smiled. "The last vile we bought worked. And I know I didn't tell you first but I wanted to see for myself."

I covered my mouth. Nikki and me had been paying thousands of dollars for a nigga's spunk because I didn't want her fucking her ex-boyfriend who was always laying in wait. Just like her I wanted a baby but we tried so many times at the IVF clinic that I stopped asking if it worked. I just assumed it didn't.

"Aren't you happy?" She asked me. "All of the heartbreak and it finally paid off. We gonna be parents."

I eased out of bed, jumped into my jeans and walked toward my dresser to grab the bottle of Hennessey. My back was faced her direction. "You my baby so of course I'm happy." To be honest I didn't know what I felt.

I didn't want her to see the sour look on my face. I mean I know we planned this shit, and I know I'm playing myself but she didn't prepare me for what it would be like to really be a father. We're together almost every day and now she was pregnant and saying she was leaving. Which I still didn't understand.

I could hear her breathing heavily behind me like she was about to cry and I felt bad. She's probably worried that I'ma be like one of these niggas and leave her stranded.

So I pulled myself together, got rid of the craziness in my mind and when I was good, I turned around and faced her. Her expression was stuck, like she needed me to be excited before she could celebrate.

"Are you sure you happy, Tasha," she asked walking up to me, rubbing my back. "Because it don't feel like that right now."

"Nikki, we wanted this but why you gotta go?" I paused. "Don't you want this with me?"

"Yes. Of course I do!" She paused. "You helped me pay for this and—"

"So why you leaving?"

"Because we can't do this, raise a baby, in Adamsville."

I took a deep breath. I knew she wanted more. "So what you want me to do?"

"Come with me." She said. "Come with us, Tasha. Leave all this craziness behind in Adamsville. We deserve more and you know it. I'm begging you."

Loud banging at the door interrupted us. "Tasha, come out here, ma stabbing herself in the hand again," Crystal yelled. "I need your help!"

CHAPTER THREE
CRYSTAL

My mother is in her pink cotton panties in the middle of the living room acting a fucking fool. I hated this kind of shit. "Ma, you can't be playing with the knife!" When the knife hung low I rushed her, knocking her to the living room floor. Nikki grabbed the knife while I tried to pin her down but it was a lot of work. "What the fuck is wrong with you, ma? Please stop!"

Her legs are wide open and I can see her bushy pussy. "Get off me, Crystal!" She yelled. "Don't put your hands on me!"

"Ma, you can't be out here like this!" I continued trying to talk to a mad woman. "We got company and everything! Please stop!"

"Get your dyke ass off me!" She yelled. "Get your god damn hands off of me, whore." She paused. "I done told you time and time again to stop touching me and you won't listen."

"Where is her medicine?" Tasha asked helping me hold her. "And what you do to set her off? Because something had to happen."

"I don't know." I said honestly putting all the pressure I could on her body. "It's like it happened from no where."

"Well where were you when she first went off?" She looked down at her. "Because she doesn't go from zero to one hundred without a reason. Even without her medicine."

"One minute she was watching the Real Housewives of whatever and the next minute she was cursing and talking about rent money. I was outside paying the mobile repairers to fix our car window." I paused. "And when I came back Lil' Kevin was barking and trying to get away from her. I think she stepped on him or something and the barking may have set her off."

Moms suffered from bipolar disorder and if she doesn't take her meds, she's a mess like right now.

Tasha stood up and took the knife from Nikki's hand throwing it on the table. Then she came back down to help me hold our mother again. "Nikki, go into ma's room and bring that yellow pill bottle on the dresser." She said. "It should be by her perfume."

"I don't want no bitches in my fucking room, I done told ya'll niggers that before! Somebody stealing from me!"

Tasha shook her head. "Ain't nobody stealing from you, ma. How many times do I have to tell you that?" She took a deep breath. "I can't with all this shit."

"Go 'head, Tasha," I told her. "You go find it because I got her and she ain't getting up."

She held her feet as we both still struggled. "Nah, I'm staying right here, Crystal. The last time I let her go when she was like this she got away from you and ran down the block and started knocking on neighbors doors. Almost got shot and everything." She looked at her girlfriend. "Do it for me, bae."

"I got it," Nikki said rushing into my mother's room before I could dispute.

I glared at Tasha as Nikki walked away. "You smell like pussy," I said to her as my mother continued to wiggle under me. "You a mess."

"I can't keep doing this," Tasha said looking at ma. "I can't keep living like this. Shit gotta change."

I looked at ma and back up at her. "We can talk about this later."

Tasha nodded but something was different. I just couldn't figure out what. I guess we were both tired of goin' through this type of drama. All our lives our mother has been unstable. If she's not changing moods at the drop of a dime, she's leaving the house for days and making us worry that someone killed her. I know Tasha wanted out of Adamsville just as much as I did and I knew one day we would go together. But only when the time was right.

"I brought two bottles because I wasn't sure," Nikki said to me. She held them up so I could see them. This a stupid whore.

"If one bottle is yellow and the other bottle is red, which one you think I want?" I asked her.

"Don't disrespect," Tasha said taking the bottle from her. "She didn't have to do shit, Crystal."

I rolled my eyes.

After we forced three pills down mama's throat, we sat with her on the brown sofa and waited for her to get better. While waiting, I cleaned her knife scratches and put a bandage on them. Before long she wasn't moving as much and her eyes focused on us instead of everything else. The doctor said she only needed a pill a day, but she didn't know our mother like we did.

When she finally calmed down Lil' Kevin jumped into my lap. I carried him to the kitchen and Tasha and Nikki followed. "Ya'll might need to have her checked out again," Nikki said. "She seems to be getting worse to me."

LEVEL UP 51

"Bitch, shut the fuck up," I waved her off. "You don't know shit about her. Stay in your fucking place."

"Crystal, I love this one," Tasha said to me. "So be careful how you talk to her."

I looked at Nikki and rolled my eyes. Taking a rubber band off my wrist I tied my long hair up in a bun on top of my head. "Yeah, whatever. She's your whore not mine."

I was about to walk away when Tasha said, "Come ride with me right quick. I got something to tell you that can't wait."

"Where we going?" I asked.

"This important." She kissed Nikki. "Watch my mother, bae. She should be good now. We be back."

We hopped in our car and drove to our old high school. I parked and sat on the hood while Tasha leaned against the car. "I'm leaving." She said without even giving me a warning.

My eyes widened and I slid down. "Leaving where?"

"Away."

"So hold up, you not even gonna tell me where you going?" My long hair fell out of the bun on it's own and I quickly wiped it out of my face.

"Nikki pregnant, Crystal. And I can't have our kid around ma especially when she like this." She paused. "I can't even believe that after all this time she still tripping. I mean, what the fuck? I hate not knowing what mood she gonna be in each day."

"She getting old," I said. "So now we gotta realize—"

"I ain't gotta realize shit," Tasha said louder. "I'm out. And there ain't much more to say."

My heart thumped in my chest and I walked in front of her. "What about us being together forever? What about the house we were going to buy?"

"You got, Tiffani."

"Ain't nobody being together forever with no Tiffani. You saw how crazy she was." I paused. "It's me and you like we talked about when we was kids. Now if she wanna come along—"

"It's me and Nikki, Crystal." She said looking into my eyes. "Ain't you been listening to me?" She asked scratching her wild curly hair. "I'm out of Adamsville."

Tasha was still talking but I didn't hear her anymore because I was getting angrier. I focused on her eyes because I want to see if this was the same bitch who told me she would never leave my side, especially after all we went through as kids. She was my best friend. The only one I could really depend on. I wanted to see if she was the same one who said we would always take care of each other because that's what sisters do.

"You really gonna abandon me, Tasha?" My breath grew heavier. She doesn't respond. Just turned her head away. "Don't you see what Nikki's trying to do, Tasha? Bitches like that don't like sisters being together. They not use to the type of bond we have because it's rare. Two gay sisters in the same house," I laughed. "We a phenomenon." I paused. "Please don't let her do this to us. We the Burton Sisters and this ain't what family do to each other."

"I need that woman, Crystal. It's not just her but the baby too. If I do right by her we can build the family I dreamed about and the house I see when I close my eyes at night." She paused. "Shit, maybe after awhile you could come live with us and we can open the business we always talked about since I know how much you love dogs." She smiled. "But all that shit goes out of the window though if I let her get away."

"You sound just like that bitch of yours." I said. "Selfish."

"Crystal, you my sister, but I told you I love her. Please don't keep calling her out her name."

I'm so angry right now that when I tried to open my mouth my lips don't even move. Fuck this dyke! If she wanted to let Nikki come in between us then that's on her, not me. Blood is richer than cum but I guess she don't get that. "What about this," I paused. "Let's do one more job and—"

"No. I'm out of that game too."

I was trembling with rage. Now she was violating in so many ways. "You know what, Tash, I'm out here in the world on my own 'cause of you. And if something happens to me, like I get raped or something, then remember this day right here." I pointed at the ground. "Because it will be all on your head." I got into the car and rolled out, leaving her right there.

CHAPTER FOUR
TASHA

When Crystal left me at the school I had Nikki come scoop me up in an old silver Honda Accord that I only used when I wasn't in dad's car. I bought it from this chick that wanted to fuck me a while ago, which gave Nikki another reason to hate it. Other than that it ran okay but above all it was all mine. I didn't have to share it with my sister.

Nikki and me were riding around trying to find Crystal so that I can talk some sense into her so she wouldn't be mad at me. Or, to kiss her ass as Nikki called it. We been up and down the streets of Atlanta and every time I'd pass a girl with a fat ass and long hair I would get annoyed when it wasn't her. I mean, why she gotta act fucked up just 'cause I wanna better life?

"I can't believe your sister doing this to you," Nikki said looking out her window as I drove. "This so juvenile. She knew she was goin' to upset you and that's exactly what she did. Didn't she? You mad right?"

"You know how Crystal is, Nikki. She wear her feelings on her sleeve but she'll come around like always." I pulled up on some red female wearing a similar outfit but once again it wasn't her. "Yep, Crystal will come 'round."

She looked at me with an attitude. "So it really doesn't matter that she does this kind of shit all the time?" She paused. "Open your eyes because it's right in front of you."

"What you getting at?" I felt my temples thumping and the last thing I wanted was to get mad at her.

"Are you having second thoughts about leaving? 'Cause if you are you need to rethink our relationship too." She brushed her long hair out of her face. "Crystal been pulling this shit since the first day I met you. It's like I'm competing with her or something. Whenever she can't get her way she tries to make you feel guilty. Sooner or later you're goin' to have to cut ties, baby."

My jaw tightened. "Do I tell you to cut your family off, even though your uncle steals out your purse every payday? " I looked at her seriously. "Do I tell you to ignore your friends when they be posting your business online just to get you mad because you don't come around?"

She frowned. "Hold up, Tasha, that's—"

"Do I, Nikki?" I interrupted her. "Or do I respect you for your own decisions because they are your own decisions?"

"You're right." Her head hung low. "I just hate seeing you like this and it's only because I care about you." She paused. "We together, Tasha. And this is the kind of thing couples do I guess."

"You know why I don't get in your business?" I continued ignoring her last comment. "I don't step in because that's your life like this is mine. So if I can respect you why the fuck can't you respect me?"

"Because I'm scared for you, Tasha." She paused. "Crystal has proven that whenever she can't get her way things go from bad to worse. And all I'm saying is that you should prepare for it. I know her. She will start drama just to get you to stay around. I wouldn't be surprised if it happened tonight."

"You don't need to be scared for me," I shrugged. "I'm a grown ass woman and I can handle whatever comes my way, even if it involves my sister. Plus I been doing this for years."

She took a deep breath. "You know what, I'ma be honest. I'm scared you're not goin' to go with me and get away from here. That's what I'm really worried about."

She may be right. I looked out ahead and sighed. I remembered the dream my sister had about us getting a new house and living a better life together. If I left Crystal right now, she would do this type shit all the time, except I wouldn't be around to help. "Why you trying to leave so bad anyway? We can raise a kid at our—"

"Nah, we can't!" She shook her head quickly from left to right. "We can't stay here so don't even say it." She paused. "I mean, are you really ready to risk losing me? Because do or die I'm gone."

I'm done arguing with her. "Aye, Nikki, let it go. Trust me. I'm getting mad now."

She looked at me with evil eyes. "You really don't give a fuck do you?" I ignored her. "You know what, stop the car, Tasha."

I don't. Nikki does this shit all the time and she got the nerve to be talking about my sister being petty. In the past we'd get into an argument and when she couldn't get her way she'd threaten to jump out. Just like Crystal. It's like I'm dealing with the same female. I'm trying to find my sister and I don't have time for this right now so I keep it moving.

"Tasha, I'm not fucking around. Stop the car." I wanted her to know this time was different than the rest because she'd done this before. "Either stop or I'm jumping out I swear to God."

"Aye, Nikki, if I pull this car over I'm not kissing your ass this time." I paused. "I'm done and you gonna be walking these dark ass streets alone. I hope you realize that." I looked over at her.

"Nigga, you don't have to do shit but leave me the fuck alone," she yelled smacking me on my right cheek while I'm driving. "I ain't asking you to kiss my ass, bitch. Be gone!"

This bitch gonna make me kill her! I'm so sick of her hitting on me. Now if I cracked her jaw open like a nut I'd be wrong. Instead of laying hands on her and being as ignorant as her I pulled over in front of a liquor store to grant her wish. At least she wasn't in the dark.

But instead of getting out she looked at me. "Tasha, you need to make a decision right here and right now." She pointed down. "Either you gonna have this baby with me or it's over between us tonight. Because I'm not gonna spend the rest of my life trying to compete with your sister. I'm done with all the games. So what's it gonna be?"

I looked over at her. I don't say anything at first because I want to stare at her pretty face for as long as I can. When I got the mental picture I said, "Get out, bitch, we done."

The tears filled up in her eyes. After awhile they rolled down her face and she made sure I saw it all. "You really want me to walk out of your life forever, Tasha? Can you really handle it?"

I turned toward my window. I can't look at her anymore. "Bounce, Nikki. I got more important things to do, like find my sister."

When she got out I pulled off before she could change her mind. I could hear her cries halfway up the block but I don't stop these wheels. When I couldn't see her body anymore I remembered niggas and bitches get robbed around there all the time. As a matter of fact it was a place Crystal and me went to rob people whenever we wanted a little extra cash.

My heart tugged and I was tempted to go back and look for her but Nikki and these ultimatums put me on some vengeful shit. She can't come between me and my sister no matter what. And if I go back that means I'm letting her do just that.

I was driving for an hour and I still couldn't find Crystal. She wouldn't answer her phone either, so, there's that part. I figured she'd come home whenever she was ready. So I officially called my search off.

Since I didn't feel like goin' home myself, because I'm not trying to be around Tiffani who hung around so much she thought she lived there, I decided to call Carmen, a girl I met at the mall when I was getting some clothes a while back. I took my phone out my pocket and dialed her number. When I heard her voice I said, "Carmen…what's up with you tonight?"

"Hey, sexy, if you game I'm fucking your pretty ass." She said. "So please tell me you on your way."

I smiled. I got a fetish for women who say what's on they minds. "That's what I'm calling you about. But for real, what you over there getting into?"

"Nothing that can't be stopped if you give the word." She paused. "So again, are you coming or not?"

"You talk a lot of shit." I grinned.

"I speak gospel. I just wish you finally choose me but that's for another day." She paused, probably sensing I didn't feel like this type of conversation again. "I can cook you up some spaghetti too. Throw some buttermilk biscuits in the oven and everything. Just the way you like."

"And why would you do all of that for me?"

"Because I'm extra horny and you a greedy fine ass dyke who needs her energy." She laughed. "Plus I know how it is when we done. You like to eat." She paused. "Crystal not with you though is she?"

Crystal normally hung around so I guess she didn't feel like dealing with her just like the world. "Nah. It's just me and you tonight." I turned my car around so I could hit the interstate. "I guess I'll be at your spot in forty minutes then."

"See you soon," she hung up.

I took 75 to get to her house while sipping a little vodka from the liquor store I stopped by earlier. Everything that happened today played out in my head on repeat. It wasn't even two hours and already I'm missing Nikki. If I let her go she'd probably meet some lawyer type bitch who just as pretty as her. Or she may even get back on dick again. I guess it's for the best. We two different people and maybe I can't compete. At the end of the day I was a hood bitch who liked hood shit.

When I make it to Carmen's house I'm thrown off when I squinted my eyes only to see Nikki sitting in the back of an Uber. She got out of the car and stood in front of Carmen's brownstone. My heart dropped in my lap because I didn't know she knew anything about Carmen let alone her address.

I parked, got out and approached her quickly. This girl wild as fuck. I mean how she get here before me? And how she know where I was going? "What you doing out here?"

I can tell she'd been crying since I left her. "I thought about what you said, about not coming between you and your sister. And my decision goes like this, Tasha, I can't live without you." She walked closer. "I tried but I don't think it's possible."

"Nikki, what you—"

"Shhhh…" She placed her finger over my lips. "If you wanna make sure we get her together before we leave than that's what we'll do." She paused. "But let's be clear, Crystal aside, before I leave I will put so many bullet holes in that bitch upstairs it'll be like she never existed." She raised her shirt and showed me the gun I bought for her last Christmas. Nikki was a gun enthusiast. Fuck was I thinking? "If I can't have you, neither will she."

"Nikki, what the fuck are you doing?" I whispered since we were outside in a good neighborhood. I looked around and no one seemed to be looking at the moment anyway.

"You know exactly what I'm doing, Tasha. You brought me to this point when you started fucking with my heart." She turned around to walk up the stairs to Carmen's and I pulled her back, holding her in my arms.

"Don't do that," I hugged her tightly. I could feel the handle of the gun pushing into my thigh because she's so much shorter than me. "You too smart for this kind of shit, girl. How you sound? You trying to get locked up for life?"

"Get off, Tasha." She tried to wiggle out my grasp but I held her firmly. "I'm serious. I'm 'bout to fuck this whore up for getting into our relationship. I'm sick of all this shit."

"I'm done with that bitch, baby." I said seriously. "I was only out here to relieve some stress that's all. To be honest I'm glad you here."

"Get off of me," she said as she continued to squirm. "Because right now you sound dumb as shit. Plus I'm still mad you left me at the liquor store."

"Did you hear me?" I squeezed her and looked down at her. "I said I'm rolling with you." She looked up at me. "But you wild as shit for this move, Nikki. How the fuck you even know where I was goin'?"

"Because I let you have her, Tasha." She paused. "I been knew about her. I figured if I didn't shut down this little thing you had going on with her like you do with the other side chicks, I could find you when I needed you. And guess what, I need you now and I'm here. But if you think I'm gonna let that bitch take you away you got another thing coming."

I kissed her lips, grabbed her ass and pulled her toward me again. "Nikki, if we gonna do this thing you gotta let me handle my family my way. It ain't for you to manage that situation with Crystal. It's on me. And stop putting your hands on me before I fuck you up. Besides, you need to stay calm. You pregnant now and can't be on no dumb shit anyway."

"Okay, baby." She smiled hugging me tighter. "Whatever you say."

Man, this girl on some wild shit. I shook my head. When my phone vibrated in my pocket and I read

Crystal's message my heart dropped. "What is it, Tasha? Is everything okay?"

"We gotta go," I looked down at her. "Crystal was just stabbed!"

CHAPTER FIVE
CRYSTAL

(AN HOUR EARLIER)

I'm on top of Mercy with my clit firmly on her pussy while Tiffani is underneath us licking and sucking anything she could. At the moment, the little problem I had between my legs wasn't bothering me, which I was grateful about. I could feel my blood making my pussy juicier as I rubbed on her. This shit was beyond steamy and I'm surprised Tiffani went along with my plan for a threesome especially after all that shit she did earlier breaking my car window.

Maybe it was guilt. Or something else. I guess when I called her out on not being willing to do anything I wanted to please me, she figured she'd better give me what I wanted, even if it meant letting me fuck her friend.

"Mmmmm," Mercy moaned biting on her bottom lip before grabbing my right titty and sucking. "That shit feels so good." My long hair brushed against her face as I watched her lick.

Mercy is definitely a sexy girl with her big breasts and fat ass. She's just my speed and I lied when I told Tiffani I wasn't interested. Not too skinny or fat but big enough for me to rub my pussy on. I don't know what my real obsession with Mercy is about but if I'd have to guess I'd say she was the only bitch I went after but couldn't get. Until today.

And I needed this shit too. After I got into it with my sister and told Tiffani I was stressed she agreed to the threesome and called her friend. Her only condition was that I didn't look into Mercy's eyes while I was on her. Her request was easier said than done because she was so right. And sex was so much better when you stared into each other's eyes.

"Damn, Crystal," Mercy whispered. "Your pussy feeling so juicy and right. Keep it right there, sexy."

I lowered my eyes and shook my head, to warn her not to talk while fucking. I didn't want Tiffani thinking her and me would hook up again without her if the sex was too good which was definitely on my mind.

Mercy whispered, "But I can't help it." She smiled at me like she was trying to start shit and cum at the same time. "You so fucking pretty. And I love looking at you."

"Eat my pussy from the back, Crystal," Tiffani said. I wondered if she heard her. "So I can lick Mercy." She paused. "Plus I feel like a toilet down here. I mean who gonna hook me up? I been doing all the work."

SHIT! Tiffani blowing me! I fucked her on a regular so it ain't like we don't do our thing at home. I kinda wanted to glide on Mercy a little longer but if I said anything other than okay, Tiff would turn it into a whole different situation. And the last thing I wanted was another fight for tonight.

Tiffani was a Dom but she acted like a bitch, which sometimes turned me off. I was used to the Dom women in my life being more aggressive but that wasn't the case with her. To be honest in my opinion she was a soft Dom but she got mad whenever I gave her that title.

To appease my girlfriend I made a quick transition. Mercy was still lying face up while Tiffani crouched in front of her and ate her pussy. I was under Tiffani and sucking on her clit from the bottom.

While I'm sucking Tiffani's pussy I take my finger and play with my own. While I'm rubbing myself I'm thinking of how pretty Mercy looked when I was on top of her and before long I'm moaning hard. Although Mercy is moaning too, I could tell the way she looked at me moments earlier that she wanted me back on top of her.

It's official. Mercy is so fucking sexy that I can't wait for us to get together without Tiffani. So we could have more private time. She knew how to move her body and because she was a little thicker, there was more for me to hold onto.

Tiff must've felt me and Mercy made a connection because all of a sudden she bore down on my face making it hard to breathe. As if she wants to kill me or something. Her actions immediately make me refocus on her, and I'm reminded about how sweet her pussy tastes too. Trying to regain focus, I grabbed Tiff's ass cheeks and ram my tongue into her pussy hole. I'm just about to cum from playing with my own self when Tiffani bore down harder.

"Mmmmmmmmm," I moaned when I finally cum. "Fucckkkkk, that felt sooo good." I bit my bottom lip, secretly not wanting the sensation to stop. "This was everything I imagined and more."

Sweat from my breasts rolled on the bed. We untangled ourselves and I lie in the middle of them with Mercy on my left and Tiffani on my right. I was in erotic ecstasy.

Rubbing my stomach I said, "Mercy, what you got to eat?" I could feel my insides swirling. "A bitch hungry as fuck, especially after all that." I grinned at them both.

"Anything you can think of that you feel like eating?" She asked. "Because I keep a stocked fridge at all times. Tiffani knows that." That was probably why she was thick.

I smiled. "Cool, you should go make us some sandwiches or something." I suggested. "I can eat anything. I'll let you pick it."

She hopped up and I got a chance to look at her body again. A small line of hair ran down her pussy and I bit my lip remembering how it felt when I was pressed against her moments earlier. But when I looked to my left Tiff is in my face, frowning. She loved messing up the moment.

"You want me to make you a fried fish sandwich?" Mercy slipped into an oversized white t-shirt. "I got some beer too but I must warn you in advance, I'm known for my cooking. You gonna be hooked after this shit trust me."

"Mercy, you can kick back for a minute." Tiffani jumped up. "I don't want nobody cooking for my bitch but me...no offense though." She slid into her sports bra, boxers and sweat pants before walking out the room. "And don't be back here fucking either," Tiffany yelled. "I'm serious 'bout mine."

When she left I pulled Mercy toward me and kissed her. After that I reached over to her, slipped my hand between her legs and played with her pussy. Her clit was fat as fuck. Knowing that Tiffani could come back at anytime and kill us made me hornier.

Loving the feeling, Mercy bit down on her bottom lip and slipped her finger into my pussy. Now here we were, fingering each other on the bed. I was so horny that it doesn't take me long to cum again. When I came, I wiped my pussy with the hand towel on the floor and she threw on her panties like we were chilling. When we were done we tried to act like we didn't just fuck again.

"Why you tell Tiffani I called you?" I asked seriously. It had been on my mind even when we were fucking but I put it to the side. "Especially if you were gonna give me the pussy anyway?"

She shrugged. "I don't know…I guess I was mad." She placed a strand of my long hair behind my ear. For a second she just looked at me. "Why are you so, so aggressive but pretty?"

I laughed. "Why you skipping the subject? You got me confused, Mercy." I looked at the door to be sure Tiff wasn't coming back. When I heard the front door open and closed I figured Tiffani ran to the car right quick. Either that or she was trying to catch her best friend and me in the act by pretending to leave the apartment. "Why you tell her?"

"I don't know why," she shrugged again. "I mean Tiffani kept saying how much you love her and how you would never look at another girl." She sighed. "I guess it made me jealous to think that you were all serious about her. After you faked that last time I saw you like you wanted me."

"Look, I don't know about all that but it's like this." I exhaled. "I want to fuck you on the side but I want to keep it between us. Is that something you can handle?"

"Nah, I'm good," she said shaking her head from left to right. , "I rather keep what we got going on right here. No disrespect but I prefer as little drama as possible in my life."

I combed my long hair with my fingers to push it out my face. "Why you playing hard to get, Mercy? The way you were doing your thing just now showed me that you into me."

She shrugged. "I got my reasons."

The front door opened again and Tiffani came back a few minutes later with food for all three of us. At first I was trying to figure out what was up with Mercy. But when I realized it doesn't matter I dropped it. It's evident that she wanted me even if she faked like she didn't.

Things were silent. We were eating and for some reason I thought about my sister. I wondered where she was and if she was safe. I knew I shouldn't have left her but the decision she was making to leave me alone was selfish. Especially after we already planned our futures.

"What you thinking about," Tiffani asked while drinking beer. She was always in my business. "You look mad about something."

I took a deep breath. "It ain't nothing I'm gonna tell you about." I paused. "So just leave it alone."

"You thinking about Tasha again right?" She continued, still pushing the subject. "I can always tell when something's on your mind so there is no use in lying."

"I just don't know why she having a baby with a bitch she ain't make," I said. "It ain't like its her real baby. Now all of a sudden she gotta leave me with ma by myself."

"Maybe she trying to start a family," Tiff said while chewing. "Don't you want something better for us? If you ask me I kinda fuck with Tasha for getting away from Adamsville but that's just me."

I don't give a fuck about wanting something better with you, bitch. "That's not what I'm saying, Tiff." I took a deep breath and raised my hand. "You know what, for real, don't even speak on it anymore. It's my business anyway."

It's quiet for a while until Mercy said, "Oh, I almost forgot." She pointed at Tiffani. "Did you tell her about that bitch who hit on you upstairs? That was some crazy shit. That whore didn't even know if we were together."

I looked at Tiffani and frowned. "What happened?"

"It was dumb," she said waving me off. "I don't even know why Mercy bringing it up anyway." Mercy grinned but Tiffani glared at her.

"Really, Tiff?" I paused. "We playing like that? I asked you what happened? Why you holding out?"

"The girl said she been wanting me for awhile and when I told her I had a girl she said not if she kicked your ass." She waved the air. "It's all dumb which is why I didn't tell you. Anyway, so I—,"

"Nah, I ain't feeling that." It was petty and I knew it but I had a lot of anger with no place to put it. I jumped into my jeans and then the rest of my clothes. I heard them begging me to leave it alone and Tiffany even picked me up until I bit her shoulder and she let me go.

By the time they caught up with me I was barefoot in the hallway. I was ready to go off on somebody and I didn't care who it was. Irritated by the world I really needed this release. "Which door is it?" I asked them.

"301," Mercy said with a sly smile on her face. It was like she knew something I didn't. "Upstairs. But what you gonna do though?"

I'm at the door banging real hard within ten seconds. I don't know her name or who I'm looking for but the moment the door opens some bitch weighing five hundred pounds it looked like came out.

Since my plan was to hit the first person I saw that's what I did. I punched her in the face and before long she stabbed me in the side. It was like she was expecting me. Tiffany knocked her to the ground while Mercy ran away.

Slut.

As I'm holding my side on the dirty hallway floor I'm trying to think how I let myself get into this anyway. Why didn't I see the kitchen knife she had in her hand? It definitely was large enough.

Now it's too late.

CHAPTER SIX
TASHA

I was yelling at the officer at the front desk in the police department because I didn't understand if my sister was stabbed why she in jail. But it's obvious he could care less because he ain't trying to help me.

"Sir, you have to tell me what's goin' on." I said. "I was told my sister was stabbed and I don't understand why she ain't in a hospital. No disrespect but you act like you don't care."

The officer looked at a stack of papers in front of him. "And like I told you before, when I find out what's goin' on I'll let you know. But you can't make me tell you anything before then." He paused. "Keep pressing the matter and you'll be able to see for yourself when I lock your ass up too. Now have a seat before I lose my patience."

"You white—" I was about to call the officer every name in the book until Nikki pulled my arm.

"Don't do this, Tasha," she whispered. "Let's just sit and wait to see what happens. "Please, baby. The last thing you wanna do is go off on these people." She touched her belly. "And if you do that I'm gonna have to get involved and what about the baby?"

I looked at the officer and back at Nikki. I decided to calm down because she's right. If I'm locked up I can't help my sister or Nikki for that matter. But my heart felt like it was about to jump out my chest because I always knew what was goin' on with my sister. And Crystal predicted something might happen to her and she was right. Why did I let her leave earlier tonight?

Extremely nervous, I sat in one of the hard plastic black seats across from the officer. I'm staring him down waiting for something. "She's okay," Nikki said softly, placing her hand over mine. "Try not to worry too much, Tasha. Plus Crystal is tough."

"You don't understand, Nikki." I turned to face her. "She just told me if anything happened to her it would be my fault. And now she gets stabbed? How can I not carry this load on my heart?"

LEVEL UP

She shook her head slowly. "What happened tonight ain't on you and you know it. Crystal got caught up in some shit and got hurt. Look at the good part, if she's here she can't be hurt badly right?" She sighed. "Just remain positive because you have a tendency to fly off the handle like you were about to with that officer. We at war with them you know."

I looked into her eyes. "Remain positive?" I paused. "Do you see what the fuck is going down now?"

"I just don't want this incident to push our plans all the way back, Tasha. That's all I'm saying. Crystal is grown with a life of her own. You have to let her do her and not get in the middle too much."

I clenched my fists because she was so super annoying. "Nikki, shut the fuck up with all this dumb shit!" I paused. "The only thing I'm thinking about right now is Crystal and her safety. That's it, and that's all."

She threw her hands up in the air and leaned back into the seat. It squeaked a little. "All I can do is be real with you, Tasha." She said under her breath. "If you want a bitch to be fake maybe I should've let you fuck Carmen after all. Sometimes I think I'm too much woman for you anyway."

I shook my head and laughed. "You always find a way to bring up the past don't you? Well I'm not biting this time."

"I'd think you'd appreciate living in the past since that's all you keep talking about. In my opinion you don't care about nothing that has to do with the future. Our future."

I'm about to walk outside and wait to get away from her when Crystal struts out of the back of the precinct. Her left side is bandaged and she's holding it. She also has blood all over her jeans.

Relieved, I stood up and she walked toward me. I gripped her into a hug and she says, "Ow, bitch!" She yelled before giggling. "That shit hurts. Let me go."

I pushed her back and observed her wound. "Should we go to the hospital? Because they said you were stabbed and the last thing you want is that shit getting infected."

"Nah, it was just a little poke that only needed two stitches." She smiled. "Trust me, I'm alright. If I wasn't I would let you know."

I looked at her feet. "Where your shoes?"

"I left 'em at, Mercy's." She sighed. "One minute I was eating and the next, well the next I was getting stabbed I guess." She laughed again. "I still can't believe everything went down like it did."

"Fuck happened, Crystal?" I looked her over. "I mean who did this shit? Give me the address so I can deal with it a.s.a.p." I paused. "Because they not getting away with this."

"Trust me, it's not worth it anyway, Tasha," she said under her breath. "And look, I'm sorry to even put you through all this. It's a complete waste of time and Tiff shouldn't have called you. I told her to get the money to bail me out but she was broke as usual." She paused. "But how you get the rest of the money? Bail was $1,000 and we only made a little."

I looked at Nikki. "She gave me the rest from what we were going to use for our move." I paused. "I know you don't like her but she definitely came through. And you should thank her."

Instead of thanking Nikki like normal, Crystal rolled her eyes at her instead. "Thanks for bailing me out or whatever the fuck," she said looking at the grungy floor. "Although I would've been aight."

Nikki returned the favor by sighing and rolling her eyes back. "Whatever, Crystal. You can keep your fake ass apology. It's not needed over this way."

"But can we talk, Tasha?" She looked over my shoulder at my girl again. "Sister to sister. Without your girlfriend?"

I looked back at Nikki and then Crystal. "Yeah, but let me rap to her right quick because we drove here together." I paused. "I still gotta find away to get her home though."

Crystal frowned at her and said, "I'll be waiting outside." I threw her the keys to my car. "Try not to be too long though, Tasha. We have a lot of things to talk about."

I walked over to Nikki and held her hands into mine. Before I could say anything she said, "Don't tell me you want me to catch a cab. When you know how much I hate them."

I frowned because she just hopped out of an Uber when she was about to fight Carmen. "Listen, I just wanna talk to Crystal. I promise I won't be long okay? I mean she did just get—"

"Cut the shit, Tasha and keep it real." She paused. "Do you want me to catch a ride or not? I don't need to hear about how vulnerable she is. I'm the one who's pregnant."

My nostrils flared. "Well I could put you in a cab or you could take the car and we catch a cab instead." I shrugged. "It's just that I have to talk to Crystal in private and if someone is driving us they might be ear hustling. She seem like whatever she wanted to tell me was important."

"It's cool. I'll grab an Uber but you need to tell your sister that I'm not goin' anywhere. And one of these days we goin' to have to get along, especially since I have plans to be your wife." She kissed me softly on the cheek. "And after you tell her that tell her I was worried about her tonight and I'm glad she's okay. I know she won't care though."

She walked away and pushed out the front door. I followed and surprisingly a cab pulled up directly in front of us before she could order an Uber. She waved, entered the cab and rode off. I walked to my car and slid inside. Crystal was waiting.

"Your bitch just threw the fuck you sign in the air when she got in the cab," Crystal said shaking her head. "I don't care what you say, I hate her. " She looked down at her wound. "But look, I don't wanna talk about her tonight." She paused. "While I was in the cell I had a lot of time to think. About a lot of stuff."

LEVEL UP 91

"You act like you did twenty years or something," I laughed. "You weren't in there that long."

"I'm serious, Tasha." She sighed. "Besides, even an hour is too much time to be in that bitch. Anyway, I thought about you leaving and I want the best for you. Sincerely."

"Wait a minute," I smiled, "What the fuck they do to you? Not even five hours ago you were giving me shit."

She shook her head and laughed. "I'm not gonna lie I did get a little mad at first but I can't stop you from doing what you want." She sighed. "I just hope your girl is real and gonna do right by you because I don't trust her."

"Let me worry 'bout her." I said. "So what did you want to talk to me about because it seemed serious?"

"Okay so it's like this." She paused and touched her side a little. "Do one more job with me, just one, and I promise I won't ask you for anything else." She paused again. "Please, Tasha. It's time to level up and get this money. But just like I'm there for you, by understanding that you want to leave Adamsville, you have to be there for me too. So what's it gonna be?"

CHAPTER SEVEN
TASHA

I was at the counter at the Post Office putting away stamp books while Crystal was singing and servicing customers. The few we had. As a matter of fact the most customers we had in a day was about eleven. She been cool all day like what we were about to do was as easy as breathing. We were waiting on the right mark.

But today feels wrong. Like I'm walking into a trap.

My stomach churned because I had a bad feeling about goin' through with our plan tonight. It feels desperate, like life or death, which is an emotion I never had to deal with before a job. Plus we didn't know who we would hit, just a few good ideas which wasn't enough.

While I was still putting up stamps, a dope dealer name Michael 'Hollywood' Lane who had a thing for Crystal walked up to her at the counter. He was all smiles and never gave up. "When you gonna let me take care of you?"

"Ain't you married?" Crystal said. "Because for some reason I remember you coming in here with your wife. Although I could be wrong."

He frowned. "Married?" He pointed to himself. "Me?" He paused and looked around as if someone was setting him up. "Who told you that shit?"

I shook my head and laughed, knowing the last thing Crystal wanted was dick. Plus I'm sure this dude really was married and it was obvious that he was willing to throw his wife under the bus. "It ain't true?" Crystal asked. "I mean you could tell the truth either which way. It probably won't matter to me anyway."

"Nah," he said calmly. He placed both palms flat on the counter. "I ain't married and I'm never gonna be married." He paused. "So now can I take you out?"

Crystal looked over at me and back at him. "How can I help you today, boy?" Crystal said putting her hand on her hips.

"You mean besides taking care of you?" He tapped the counter. "And spoiling your fine ass rotten? Something I been trying to do for months."

Crystal frowned. "You know what, I'm about to walk away from your ass. If you don't need help I'm—"

He reached over the counter and grabbed her hand. "Okay, okay, you don't have to get so serious," he paused and let her go. "I wanna stop the mail from coming to my house. Which form I gotta fill out to make that happen?"

Crystal tried not to look at me but I understood what that meant. He was going out of town, which meant we could get paid. The only thing is I was afraid to hit Hollywood's place. I knew he may have had a house in the neighborhood but he was still hood and dangerous.

Crystal gave him the form and he filled it out while talking to her at the same time. "I wish you weren't so mean," he said taking off his NY black baseball cap and putting it on backwards. "You too pretty for all that."

"Well I am mean." She crossed her arms over her chest. "And you bothering me." She paused. "So you done filling it out yet?"

He chuckled. "Alright, alright, I'ma leave you alone." He slid the form over to her. "You looked like a friendly person and I wanted a little conversation. But if you serious about not being interested I'll leave you be."

She cleared her throat. "So where you off too for vacation?"

"My auntie just died so I'm going to Texas." He paused. "Not looking forward to it at all. Not even a vacation but I still have to go." He shrugged. "What you gonna do? When family calls you have to bounce."

"Wow, I'm sorry to hear that." She said. "Don't you have anybody to house sit?" Crystal continued. "Because these forms can sometimes not really work.

Which means you'll get a lot of mail in your box anyway."

"Like I said I'm single," he winked at her and pushed the form toward her. Crystal accepted it and keyed in the information. "Although I don't want it to stay that way."

"Single for now I'm sure," Crystal said blushing. "If you keep up with your persistence I'm sure you'll be bae'd up in no time."

"Come on," he said playfully putting his hand on hers again as she keyed in his address. "Let me take you out when I get back. I know I been getting on your nerves but I'm really interested in you. Plus you look familiar. Like I've seen you some place else. And not just in here. Maybe in my dreams."

Crystal sighed. This dude was way corny. "You know what you've worn me down." She paused. "So when you coming back?"

He tapped the counter again as if he finally got what he wanted. "Next Friday."

Crystal looked at me and back at him. "Well, when you get back give me a call." She wrote her number down. "We'll start from there."

"Damn, you made my day." He knocked on the counter again. "And I look forward to making that call." He winked and walked out, taking one last look at her before he left.

When he was gone I walked over to Crystal. "We can't fuck with it! That nigga is dangerous, I'm telling you. Plus you been giving him shit and all of a sudden you interested. If something happens to his house he's gonna suspect us immediately." I shook my head from left to right. "We gotta leave it alone."

"No we don't," she said grabbing my hands. "This is the one that will probably give me enough money to live by myself. That way you can go on with your life, Tasha." She picked up the Address Forward card, looked at it and inhaled. "Trust me this is the one. The big one."

"You not even listening, Crystal. The man will suspect you first if he gets robbed. You did way too much by asking who was house sitting. The shit is off and we done."

"Well, what about me, Tasha? You making decisions without even thinking about where I'm gonna be when you run off into the sun with Nikki."

"Are you listening to yourself?" I asked. "You sound like a lunatic out here."

"No, are you listening to yourself?" She pointed at me. "If we don't do this job how the fuck am I gonna take care of the family? How am I gonna take care of ma? I mean I know I got this job but we both know with her insurance it ain't enough for her meds. You abandoning us, Tasha and you wrong as fuck for that shit."

"You act like you gonna get a million dollars from this dude!" I repeated. "This is a dangerous move and I don't like it at all."

"It don't matter how much we get, Tasha! As long as we get something." She paused. "What I do know is that you getting all scared for nothing. This could be the biggest job we've ever had. And you ready to let it go."

"You heard what I said right, Crystal." I paused looking at her with narrow eyes. "The shit ain't up for discussion, I'm sorry."

"I heard you but what if I don't wanna listen?" She crossed her arms over her chest. "What if I do the job by myself? Or with Tiffani? It ain't like I need you to get that money anyway. I've done plenty by myself before."

"If you rob that nigga you don't have shit else to say to me." I was completely serious. "I'm not even playing around with you. This would be the end of our bond."

"Well I'm gonna get it anyway. And if something happens to me that's on you." She walked toward the back of the office.

CHAPTER EIGHT
TASHA

I let my sister rope me into some dumb shit once again. If Nikki knew what I was about to do she would be livid.

I'm sitting in the passenger seat of a stolen car, dressed in all black smoking weed while Crystal drives. I got a lot of shit on my mind and I was in no mood to be robbing some trap nigga who was away at a funeral. But I couldn't have Crystal going by herself either. She knew that about me which made me hate this situation even more.

And then there's this baby shit with Nikki. I'm not sure, but I don't know if moving away is for me. I mean, what if Crystal's right? What if Nikki is foul? Not only that but she hasn't been answering my calls since I put her in a cab that day. Where she at?

I didn't just hit her house phone and her cell, I also called her best friend who does closures at a salon and she claimed she hadn't seen her either. Any other time she'd be burning my cell phone up and I'd have to put her off but not today. She was definitely acting different.

"Still trying to call that bitch huh?" Crystal asked as she steered the car down the street. "That chick really do got you on some soft shit. I swear, out of all of the bitches you came across I couldn't see her being the one." She shrugged. "If you ask me Carmen way badder than her but that's just my opinion though. What do I know?"

I shook my head. She's calling her multiple bitches to get me mad but I don't bite this time. Plus once again she not saying shit I wanna hear or talk about. "So you speaking to me now?" I asked. "Because you ain't have no words for me earlier. When I said I wasn't going."

"I never wasn't speaking to you, Tasha." She wiped her long hair out her face. "I just don't like you faking like you don't want this money. Like this is not what we do for a living. We robbers. Embrace that shit!"

"If by faking you mean keeping us outta prison it's whatever. Don't forget you just got out of jail a minute ago. You got court next month and already you on your goon shit. You trying to add breaking and entering to your list too? What's wrong with you?"

"Yeah, whatever." She held her head up and continued to drive. "That shit ain't gonna stand. I be surprise if that bitch even shows up. As far as her fat ass knows I'm on some get back shit. Plus it ain't like I don't know where she lives."

When my phone rung I saw who was calling and shook my head. First I put out the weed and answered. "Fuck you been, Nikki?" I paused. "I been hitting your phone all day."

"What you want?" She asked with an attitude. "Because just like you don't feel like the drama I don't either. I been having morning sickness all morning."

"First off you the one calling me." I corrected her. "So I should be asking you the same thing."

"That's because you been ringing my phone like you crazy and unlike you I got shit to do too." She paused. "Like get ready to be a mother. A single mother at that."

I looked at the phone. "You got a split personality. Has anybody ever told you that because it's true?"

"I'm just saying if you—"

I hung up on that bitch. I didn't feel like her shit right now because of what we were about to do. If she wanted to come at me like that we done. As long as I know she's safe I'm good with everything else. When my phone rung again, I ignored it . It's not until she calls me five more times that I finally answer again.

"What you want?" I put my right foot on the dashboard and took a deep breath. Before putting the weed out in the ashtray. "I thought our conversation was over since you don't know how to talk to me."

"Why you keep hanging up," Nikki said crying. "You...you don't"—she sniffled — "You don't

LEVEL UP

understand how you make me feel. I want the best for you, Tasha. I don't want you robbing niggas to—"

"Whoa!" I yelled putting my foot down. "All that on the phone? Are you crazy or just trying to get me locked up?"

"Do you remember what happened last year when you…uh went to your aunt's house?" She paused and sounded as if she was about to cry. "Because for me it was as if it just happened yesterday. I knew it was all over for you."

I think she talking in code but I couldn't be sure. This pregnancy was definitely messing up her thought process. One thing for sure, after this if we worked out, I wanted zero more children. At least not by her. "Look, Nikki, don't be doing all—"

"Do you remember or not, Tasha?" She screamed, her breath heavy as if she were on the verge of passing out. "It's a simple question and I would appreciate an answer."

I don't answer.

"She left her fingerprints in the niggas house because she used the toilet, I mean at your aunt's house." She corrected herself. "And you had to fem out because he was attracted to tall girls, pretend to meet him at the gas station and jerk him off just to get back in his house to wipe them."

I was heated. "You done being hot as fuck on the phone? Because this is way too much." Crystal looked over at me.

"Nah, are you?" She asked taking a deep breath. "Tasha, your sister gonna be the reason you get killed and or locked up."

I hung up and tucked the phone into my pocket.

"You a stupid ass bitch, Tasha. Gonna let her guilt trip you into raising a sperm baby," Crystal said under her breath. I looked over at her. "I'm not saying nothing else though. You already know how I feel about the shit but I'm just saying my part anyway."

Focusing on Nikki I said, "Like I told you a million times, I'm with her because she makes me better. And I really wanna see how far I can go with her. Let me live please."

When the car stopped a block away from the address, my sister grabbed something I couldn't see from under the seat and stuffed it under her shirt. "You ready?" She asked.

"This the place?" I questioned.

"Nah, it's the zoo," she hit me on the thigh. "Now come on. We got a job to do and the quicker we do it the better. Plus I feel like you five seconds from pulling out." She rushed out and closed the door.

I got out slowly and looked around. When I didn't see any nosey neighbors I entered the gate surrounding the property and moved toward the backyard. My heart thumped with every step I took. Why was I so nervous this time?

When I bent around the side of the house my worst nightmare was realized. Crystal was at the door holding an iron rod making excess noise. This was way off plan. I normally popped the locks and disarmed the security system because she doesn't know what she's doing.

"Move out the way so I can do it," I whispered. "Plus you not as quick as me anyway."

"If you not gonna let me try it then go back to the car." She whispered. "I gotta grow up in the game sooner or later. Since I'm gonna be by myself." She continued to make extra noise on the lock.

"Crystal, what the fuck are you doing?" I hit her in the back of the head with a closed fist and her face pressed against the door. "Move the fuck out my way!"

I contemplated grabbing her and leaving because everything tells me that goin' inside; will change the rest of my life. But she's my kid sister, and I can't let her do this shit by herself right? No matter how much I want to.

I snatched the rod from her. "Move back, I got this."

She rubbed the back of her head and then said, "Put these on first." She handed me a set of gloves and I slid them on. Within a second we're inside.

The house is really luxurious and smells of vanilla and cleaning products. We're in the kitchen so I grabbed a trash bag and stuffed everything of value I could find inside. Once I'm done we moved throughout the house to see what else we could find and I can't believe how much money and shit he has lying around this spot. Stacks of cash wrapped in rubber bands.

Already I eyed a pair of gold bamboo earrings, some chains and even a camera. I already know if we backed the car up we'd make out clean just taking everything not nailed down.

I'm in my element and things appeared to be going smoothly until I see my sister's fearful expression. "What is it?" I asked her dropping the bag. "Why you looking all crazy? The cops coming or something?"

"Don't be mad, Tasha." Her eyes widened. "I know how you are so I'm telling you right now." My heart thumped harder.

I stepped up to her. So close she couldn't move if she tried. "What the fuck is it, Crystal? Right now you got my mind going a mile a minute."

"His wife is home."

"His wife?" I repeated, mostly out of breath. "But I thought he was single?"

"Well the nigga lied." She paused. "So what we gonna do now?"

CHAPTER NINE

TASHA

I was sitting in the bedroom with Denise Lane's naked bloody body between my legs. We hadn't been in here for ten minutes and Crystal had already hit her on the head and so she was injured. Prior to that her yellow body was without a flaw so I could tell she had work done. Definitely a trap nigga's wife that's for sure.

My hand is pressed against her trembling lips and I'm squeezing so tight I can feel her teeth push back. I don't mean to be this rough but I need to keep her silent so that whoever is knocking at the door right now will go away.

One minute Crystal was saying Hollywood's wife is home and the next someone is knocking at the door. It seemed like every possible situation that could happen was happening. I knew I should've gone with my instincts and stayed home. Fuck! What is wrong with me?

Crystal stood next to the closed bedroom door with her gun looking as if she was about to blast anyone who tries to enter. I remembered when she got that piece too and I should've taken it from her then. She bought it off some chick she was fucking who was mad at her man and selling off all his stuff after she shot him in the arm with it. He survived and they got back together but still. After all this time I hoped she'd never have a reason to pull it out but I was wrong. Let's just pray it's not loaded.

"I don't hear them knocking," Crystal said with her ear pressed against the wooden door. She looked back at me. "I think we good now."

"Are you sure?"

"As sure as I'm gonna be anyway." She shrugged. "I mean, I don't hear anybody walking out there. Sounds like we in the clear. Let's just keep our voices low."

I looked down at the woman between my legs. She was frowning like she wanted to kill everybody. To be honest I can't say that I blamed her. I don't wanna hurt her more, but I needed time to think of a plan before we let her go.

"Listen, I'm gonna take my hand off your lips but if you scream I'm gonna be furious. Do you understand? And that means I'll be forced to fuck you up in here."

She nodded yes.

My hand peeled away from her wet lips slowly. Denise ran her tongue over her mouth and said, "I can't believe ya'll doing this shit." She looked at my sister and then me. "Do you know who I am? Did you even bother to do your research before coming in here?" She grabbed the sheet and covered her body before wiping the blood wound from her head.

"I know you sexy as shit," Crystal said thinking things was a joke as usual. "I can tell you that much."

"Do you have any idea about what I can have happen to you?" Denise continued looking at her and then me. "And everyone you love? This is not a game. I'm talking about your lives!"

I looked at Crystal who avoided me by looking at her instead. This is all her fault and I'm trying not to hate her because it won't help. At this point in the game I had to see the situation through.

"Denise, I know it's fucked up but we ain't trying to hurt you," I said running my hand down my face. "We just want what—"

"Not trying to hurt me?" She laughed. "It's too late for that shit because when my husband hears about this its gonna be war. Plus look at my face. I already got a cut."

"Well maybe we'll make sure he doesn't get the message then," Crystal said walking up to her with the gun aimed toward her temple. "Because if that's our only problem we won't have one if we kill you." She looked at me. "What you think, sis?"

I slapped the barrel down and it fired into the floor. I jumped off the bed and moved toward her. "Crystal, that shit loaded?"

"Yes! You thought it was a game?" She smiled. "I wouldn't come here without being strapped. This is serious business."

"Fuck is goin' on with you?" I paused. "Are you that far gone that you don't realize what's happening? We in over our heads now."

I heard the bed squeaking and looked back at Denise who managed to slip on her nightgown without us watching. Now she was staring at us with her fists clenched. When Crystal first walked in she said she caught her playing with her pussy. Anyway, she's beyond mad and has a look in her eye that could kill.

"Listen, bitches, you both cute." We looked at her. "You have your whole life ahead of you. So I'm gonna tell you like this." She paused. "You two whores get out my house right now and leave everything you bagged up and I won't tell my husband about none of this. It will be as if nothing ever happened. But if you take this option you better take everyone you love with you out of town too, because it's over for you in The A. 'Cause if I ever see either one of you in these streets ya'll done."

"And if we don't leave town?" Crystal asked. "Just what the fuck do you think you gonna do?"

"Then I guess Hollywood burying niggas for the next six months." She shrugged. "It's as simple as that." She smiled like she had the upper hand.

Before I could stop Crystal from reaching her, she comes down over her face with the butt of her gun. Again. Denise's cheek opens up and blood splashes out of her skin and drips onto Crystal and the mattress. I grabbed Crystal by the waist and tackled her to the carpet. The gun dropped out of her hand and I crawled over to it, stuffed it in the waist of my jeans and grabbed her by the shoulders.

"Get off me, bitch," Crystal yelled. She tried to push me off but I don't budge. I always have been stronger than her.

"I'm gonna really need you to calm the fuck down, Crystal!" I yelled. "You hear what I'm saying?"

LEVEL UP

"You fucked up now," Denise said smiling licking her own blood. Her white teeth turned dark red. "You'd do better putting that gun to your head than sticking around here."

Tiring of her I removed the gun from my waist and aimed at her. Now I could see Denise was scared too. "Tell me why I shouldn't kill you right now?" I cocked the gun. "Since it's obvious all is lost anyway." I shrugged.

Denise sighed and looked at the barrel. I'm not sure but something told me she knew I was serious. "There's money in here. Under the bed." She paused. "Take it. It's yours."

I looked at Crystal whose jaw was hung.

I found the money.

There had to be over one hundred thousand.

The plan was simple.

Do one more job, level up and then we'd go our separate ways. Life would be easy and me, a hood bitch from Atlanta, would get to run away with the girl of my dreams.

So why am I covered in Denise's blood? Why am I surrounded by money I ain't gonna ever get a chance to spend? And why is my sister, the one who I would give my life for responsible?

I guess we all got a story, huh? You ain't lived a good life unless somebody can look at you and say one of two things. That bitch lived hard and will never be forgotten, or I ain't ever trying to turn out like her.

For me, I guess, they gonna say both.

After finding the money and putting it in Denise's car, since we ditched the stolen one about thirty minutes earlier, I had to put Denise away. I couldn't take her taunting Crystal anymore, telling her about all of the things Hollywood was gonna do once he found out. She was only mad because she thought after giving us the money that we would go away.

She was wrong.

So she elected to talk foul. Said foul stuff like she'd cut Crystal's titties off and make dyke stew. Real terrible shit. I don't even know how she knew we were gay. I mean I looked the part but not my sister.

So we threw a black quilt over her body, duct taped her mouth and tied her to some pipes in the basement of her own house. They seemed to be sturdy and we kept walking into the basement just to make sure she hadn't gotten away. So far we were good.

We were in the master bedroom, sitting on the bed, trying to figure out our next move while Crystal was putting a fresh bandage on the stab wound on her side. I guess after we fought the stitches popped open.

"Why you pull me into this shit, Crystal," I asked her. "Just keep shit real with me. Why didn't you let me out the game when I had the chance to go? Is it because you love me or want me in hell with you?"

She looked back at me and shook her head. "Why you coming at me with this shit? Ain't this the wrong time?"

"I'm asking you a serious question," I said stepping up to her. "I'm your sister and I don't want you beating around the bush. Do you love me or not? Just be real."

"You know I do, Tasha." She said. "That shouldn't even be a question." She paused. "Don't add one thing into the other."

"Then why would you pull me in this when I had a chance to be free?" She paused. "People who love each other want the best for their family but it don't feel that way with you. I had a fucking chance, Crystal."

"There you go making everything about you again." She pushed her long hair from her face. "To be honest I thought you would love this job. I thought it would remind you about how much fun we have together. So you'll stay around."

"Fun we have together?" I repeated. "You really don't even understand what's goin' on. You got Hollywood's wife in the basement tied up." I pointed at the floor. "That woman said he killed his first victim at age thirteen by pushing a nigga off a balcony. We don't rob people like that, Crystal. We stay far away from them because we not killers."

She sighed deeply. Like I was the one who put us in this shit and she was irritated with me. "Do you love me, Tasha?" She asked crossing her arms over her chest.

"You turning this around but yes, you know I do." I paused. "That is the main reason I didn't want us doing something that could get you and me killed." I paused. "Any other questions?"

"Well if you love me, then why would you leave me alone with mama?" She was about to cry and I wasn't in the mood. "When you know the life we had coming up? Tasha, I can't take care of her without you. And what if somebody remembered what we did when we were in high school?" She asked. "Don't forget about that because I think about it everyday. If you gone I will have to deal with it alone."

"Don't try and put ma being sick on me. And that other stuff we did as kids is a done deal." I paused. "I'm the one who wanted to put ma in a place so she could get some real help."

"Well we not doing that and you know I wouldn't cosign on it. So what happens now? You gonna be somewhere with Nikki leaving me to deal with this alone. It's not fair."

My phone rung in my pocket and I was relieved because I was talking in circles. I took the cell out and walked away from her. "I gotta grab this call, Crystal." I paused. "Give me a second."

She shook her head. "I swear whenever that bitch calls you go running." She rolled her eyes. "You might as well sew your face onto her pussy. That way you can clock her every move." She stormed out the room.

"Stay away from the window," I yelled at her. "And don't forget to check on her in about an hour." I answered the phone and sat on the couch in the next room. "Hello."

"Tasha, is everything okay?" I paused. "You sounded bad when you ended the call and I've been worried. Please don't hang up on me. I can't fight anymore."

I scratched my head. "Nikki, I gotta say something but I don't want you interrupting me when I say it. It's important that you listen because I don't know when I'll be able to tell you this shit again."

"Tasha, you scaring me now." She paused. "We were arguing earlier and now you sound different. Like you about to tell me you have cancer or something else crazy."

"I know and I'm sorry. But listen." I swallowed. "I know I don't treat you right all the time. It's not because I don't love or appreciate you. It's just that sometimes I don't always do what's right. But I need you to understand that there's nobody else out there I want to be with, Nik. Yeah I used to fuck a few bitches along the way but not one of them can stand next to you and they all knew your name. That includes Carmen." I could hear her crying. "It doesn't justify my actions recently but I wanted you to know how I feel."

"This sounds like the end. And I don't know what's goin' on but unless you dead, I will always be by your side, Tasha. That's my problem and what frustrates me so much. I don't give a fuck what you goin' through. If you gotta kill somebody, I'll put my hand over yours and we'll both pull the trigger."

I smiled when I opened my eyes because I had a good night's sleep. I don't remember my bed being this soft and it felt like I'm at one of them upper class hotels in the ritzy part of Atlanta. When I smelled an unknown scent I sat up and looked down at the floor.

I wasn't at home.

Fuck is wrong with me? I was way too comfortable in this nigga's house. I guess I allowed stress to push me to sleep and didn't even realize it until now. Fuck!

Before I caught a few winks, I told Crystal who was in the basement to watch Denise while I grabbed a quick nap. Since the sun is shining into the room, I figured she let me sleep longer than I wanted and now it's the next day. The plan was to snatch some quick rest until we figured out what to do with Denise. Not be knocked out like we had no troubles.

I hopped up and saw Crystal sitting on the recliner with her head hanging back. Is this bitch actually sleep? Irritated, I walked to the front of the chair and slapped her in the face.

"What's going on with Denise, Crystal?" I looked around. "And wake the fuck up before I steal you in your jaw. You weren't supposed to let me sleep that late! You were supposed to wake me up!"

"What…who is that?" She rubbed sleep out her eyes and then yawned. "And why you talking all loud? My head hurts."

I slapped her again and her long hair fell in her face. "Whore, wake up and tell me what's going on with Denise. You were on duty and instead of watching her you out here acting like we don't have this nigga's wife."

"She's in the basement." She yawned. "And don't worry. I duct taped her a little more to the pipe. Then I tied her legs with some rope I found in the cellar. Ain't no way she moving. Trust me."

Of course I didn't believe her and I immediately rushed to the basement. When I hit the last step I saw her some feet away from the pipe, although still partially tied to it, she managed to get the duck tape up from her mouth. She was on the phone talking. I immediately snatched the handset from her and hung up. Why didn't I see the phone down here yesterday?

"Who the fuck was you talking to?" I looked down at her; the blood in my veins pumping so hard my temples throbbed. She doesn't respond. "I said who the fuck was you talking to just now on the phone, bitch?"

LEVEL UP

"You'll see," she smiled. "Yep, don't worry, you'll see soon enough."

CHAPTER TEN
CRYSTAL

Since we ditched the stolen car we were in Denise's car. Now Tasha is driving and I'm in the backseat with the gun pointed to the back of Denise's head. She may have been sexy but I hate women like her. Think just because her nigga killed a few people she powerful too. I should accidently shoot her ass. Her feet and arms are tied to the seat to prevent her from moving.

Tasha gave me back my gun because Denise was starting to be a handful. Every so often Denise would stare at the cut on her face in the window that I caused, and back at me before frowning. She could try it if she want to and I'ma open up her forehead instead.

I gotta admit, when I pictured the plan to rob his house in my mind it didn't go down like this. I just wanted Tasha to fall back in love with getting money again, the way she used to be. I figured if we took a really big job and made decent on what we stole, she would see there was no need to leave. I guess I was wrong.

"Who was that, that knocked at the door last night?" Tasha asked as she continued to drive down the street. "You might as well tell us the truth."

She shook her head. "Does it matter?" The car remained quiet.

"Yes." Tasha said.

Denise took a deep breath and said, "I ordered Chinese food before you broke into my house." Her voice was low. "So I guess it was the delivery man."

"Why didn't you tell us that last night?" I asked, looking at the bruises on her face I made from hitting her twice with the butt of the gun. "You could've made things easier."

"I didn't feel like answering your questions." She looked out the window to her right. "Just so you know, my husband knows who you are now." She laughed. "And when he gets finished with you, you'll wish you didn't exist on earth."

Tasha looked back at me and then at her. "So that's who you were talking to when I walked downstairs?" Tasha asked, with wild crazy eyes. "Your fucking husband?"

"What the fuck do you think," she laughed harder. "We been together all of our lives an he will find me." She smiled. "He's a man and if there is one thing he knows how to do is hunt bitches." She sighed. "That's been the problem in our marriage from the gate." She sighed as if she were tired of him cheating.

"Your husband ain't the only person who knows how to bust a gun, bitch," I told her. I didn't know how to use them per say but I knew how to pull a trigger and aim. In my book that was good enough. "We got guns too."

"Crystal, shut the fuck up with that dumb shit," Tasha yelled. "Let's not make the situation worse than it already is." She paused. "Plus I have to...I have to think. I just need some quiet."

"Oh...oh...so I get it," Denise said, "The butch looking one is the good one and the secret pussy eater is the bad one." She laughed. "At least you both pretty. Hollywood gonna probably fuck you both before he kills you." She chuckled. "Trust me you'll like it."

"Stop threatening us," Tasha yelled. "Now I know it's fucked up that we broke into your house and if I could let you go without worrying about our lives I would. But every time I consider pulling this car over and letting you free you remind me why I shouldn't."

Denise shook her head. "If you let me go without a plan them brown eyes of yours ain't the only things that's stupid." She laughed as if it were a game again. Suddenly I knew why Hollywood stepped out on her. She was fucking annoying.

"You know what, call Hollywood," I said to Denise. "Call him now. I don't give a fuck no more." I threw my hand up. "Plus it ain't like he don't already know what's going on to hear you tell it."

Denise turned and looked at me. "What you talking about, bitch?" She paused. "I knew you were crazy but this terrible even for you."

"Shut the fuck up with that dumb shit, Crystal." Tasha yelled from the front seat. "Ain't nobody calling nobody! What we gonna do is focus on what's happening now and—"

"Why not call him?" I interrupted her. "She said Hollywood knows who we are. Might as well talk to him and try to work some things out." I shrugged. "Financially speaking too."

"This is a bad idea, Crystal!" Tasha yelled. "Plus we have money already from this heist. Would you for once listen to me?"

"Well we could get more," I said. "I don't know if you figured it out but we already in deep shit. The least we could do is talk to him and find out what's on his mind. Maybe we can make a little better come up. "

"Like I said, I feel like this a bad idea and I'm not changing my position," Tasha continued shaking her head from left to right. "I'm telling you. This way off. I got the same feeling I had on the day we went to his house. And now look. We kidnaping his wife. I'm going with my intuition this time."

"And I feel like it's too late to do anything but try," I said. "I know you mad but you might as well let me do this."

"Now that you two bitches have come to a conclusion somebody give me the phone," Denise said with a smile on her face. I'm sure she thought this was all a joke and it made me wonder if it were the first time she'd been kidnapped. "Let's call my man and see what he has to say about this."

I dug into my pocket and handed her my cell phone. From the rearview mirror I saw Tasha looking at me. She's giving me the same look she did when I stole people's credit cards from the post office when they forgot to take them back after a purchase. She was so mad at me at one point that she ain't talk to me for a week after I stole the last one. And I'm getting the same feeling now. Like she's done with me after this.

"Hey, bae, I got them bitches right here and they want to speak to you," Denise said on the phone before looking at me. "Here she goes right here." She handed me the cell.

I took the phone from her and it shook in my grasp, but slowly I put it to my ear. "Remember me?" I looked at Tasha's face from the rearview mirror and she looked like she wanted to blow she was so mad. "Still wanna go on a date?"

"So it's a game to you?" Hollywood said. "You think I'm gonna let you do this to me and mine?"

"I don't know what you think," I shrugged. "I mean, was it a game when you lied and told me you weren't married?" I looked at Denise and suddenly she wasn't laughing anymore. "If you ask me you deserve this shit."

"If you let my wife go I swear that'll be it." He said to me. It sounded like he was running but I knew he wasn't. He was probably nervous at what was about to happen. "But you gotta do it now because my offer expires in one minute."

"You talk like you the one running shit now." I said leaning back in the seat. "If you believe that let me correct you. We running this shit and you gonna do what I say."

"Okay, I'll play." Hollywood took a deep breath. "What I gotta do, right now, to get my wife back?"

I looked at Tasha but she wasn't looking at me. I guess she was done with it all.

"Give me one million dollars." I smiled. "You a trap nigga so let's start there."

Hollywood sat in the back of his Mercedes trying to remain calm, even though his nerves were wrecked. His wife always said the females he tried to fuck would do him more harm than good, and she was right. His most loyal soldier was behind the steering wheel; with so many guns in the passenger seat he could kill a hundred people. He preferred it that way for quick access.

After getting off the phone with Crystal, he caught a flight back and was now back in Atlanta. Hollywood considered his options. "Since she has my wife do you think I could lay hands on someone she loves too?" Hollywood asked. "Of course I can," he responded to himself. He looked out the window to his right. "I wonder who she loves the most."

"Doc, show me her social page again," he said to his driver.

Doc removed his phone from his pocket while driving and handed it to him. When the phone lit up he flipped through the life of Tasha and Crystal Burton's pictures. Hollywood leaned forward and looked at Tasha's brown eyes and Crystal's smiling face. In every photo they were either posing with each other or two females.

He shook his head and handed the phone back. "What have you two bitches gotten yourself into?" He asked himself. "Life was so simple but you truly fucked with the wrong nigga this time."

"I found their address earlier," Doc said. "What you wanna do?"

LEVEL UP

"You know what needs to happen," he said. "Take me to their house. Since they fucked with my family I'll fuck with theirs."

CHAPTER ELEVEN

TASHA

I'm standing outside of the car with Crystal in a wooded area, somewhere still in Georgia, right outside Atlanta. His wife was still inside waiting on us to come back. "Crystal, why would you get on the phone and talk to that nigga 'bout his wife?"

I leaned up against the car. "I'm not understanding you right now. 'Cause the last thing we needed was this dude looking for us."

"You heard that bitch," she said pointing at Denise in the car. "He already knew. So I got news for you it's too late, Tasha, the least we can do is get some money out of it."

"You just destroyed everything I had coming to me and you don't even care." I sighed. I could see the future I planned for Nikki and me pass by and it fucked me up.

"By everything coming to you, you mean your precious bitch and sperm baby? Is that what you telling me? Because if you are, you right, I don't give a fuck, Tasha."

"You so lost right now you can't even imagine." I walked a few feet away from her, put my hands on my hips and looked up into the blue sky. "I really can't believe this is happening. Why did I approve this?"

"I'm gone," she pointed to herself. "I'm gone? At least I know who I am and I'm not letting you or some bitch named Nikki take away my identity. What about you though, huh?"

"You just put everyone in danger, Crystal. Everyone. Mama, Tiffani, everybody. You bet it all without even thinking of who you might hurt. Before you popped off with the nigga Hollywood, I had a plan to get us out of this."

"And what exactly was your plan, Tasha?"

"I was goin' to talk to Denise and try to get her to understand that we didn't mean to hurt her. And that—"

Crystal laughed and balled over, holding her stomach as if I just said the funniest thing in the world.

"Fuck is so funny?" I asked.

"I finally am able to do something for myself and you can't stand it." She paused. "But don't even mind me though. You just keep running your mouth."

"You don't know what you talking about."

"But I do," she nodded leaning on the driver's side door. Denise is still inside her car giving us dirty looks. "When this shit works out it's gonna be me who's the reason we'll never have to work again. All I wanted was a piece of the pie."

"The only thing we going to get after this is side by side caskets, Crystal." I paused. "That's it. This is the worst case scenario."

She frowned. "So what you gonna do now, Tasha?" She paused and folded her arms over her chest. "Huh? Because everything you saying ain't gonna get us out of this situation right now. Is it?"

I cleared my throat.

"Now you gonna have to have my back or walk away, grab your girl, leave town and let me do this on my own. Or help." She paused. "Because either way it's going down tonight."

I sighed and wipe my hands down my face. "Fuck!"

"I know it's wrong, but at the end of the day we in this until its over." She shrugged. "There ain't no other plan that will allow all of us to be safe without money. We either divide up now and you let me go at it alone or we stay together and you help." She moved closer. "And I really, really, need your help, Tasha. Don't you see? What you want me to do? Beg?"

I looked down at her. My heart is all fucked up because if something were to happen there would be no way I could live with myself. I knew it and so did she which is why she did wild stuff like this. "You been doing a lot of crazy shit on your own so let me ask this, is there anything else you gotta tell me?"

"What you talking 'bout," she said trying to laugh it off. "You know everything already."

"I'm serious, Crystal." I paused. "Are you being real about everything? Are there any other surprises?"

"Real huh?"

"Bitch, ain't nobody playing with you!" I yelled. "Answer the fucking question."

"Okay, okay, I'm being *real* as you so eloquently put it." Crystal laughed. "But, there is one thing." She pulled her pants down.

"What the fuck are you doing?" I looked around to be sure nobody could see us.

Before I know it she had moved closer. "You see that shit on my pussy?" She pointed at it. "I think I got

LEVEL UP 143

burned by one of my hoes. And I fucked Tiffani and Mercy the other night and I probably gave it to them too."

"Crystal, pull your fucking pants back up before I go off out here." I was so embarrassed. Not just for myself but her too. "You playing yourself real bad."

"Look at it right quick," she said. "I just need to know that whatever this shit is won't kill me."

I knew what she was trying to do. Whenever she wanted to skip the subject she would do something crazy so I would get thrown off. On the other hand when I looked from where I was I did see small bumps. "I think that's just a rash. You'll be aight." I sighed although I wasn't sure. "Now pull your fucking jeans up. You embarrassing me out here."

She does. "I guess I'll cancel my doctor's appointment. Not like I'm gonna be able to go now anyway."

"Now, is there anything else besides that disgusting shit that you have to say to me?" I paused. "I'm talking about lies or dishonesty?"

"The only thing I held back on was this weed I got in my pocket." She pulled it out and wiggled it. "I was gonna save it for an emergency, but I figure we got a life or death situation goin' on right now so we might as well..."

"You know what, light that shit up," I told her.

For fifteen minutes we smoked the bar and passed it back and forth. For that moment while we waited on word from Hollywood nothing else was goin' on in the world and Denise wasn't in the car even though she was. We talked about everything from the day we had to tell ma we were both gay to the two sisters we met in high school who we convinced to lick each other by lying about how we did the same thing.

When I was as high as I wanted, and a little more relaxed, I looked over at her. "Let's get back in the car. It's time to see where he is. I'm sure he's back in town now and everything."

Crystal opened the door and fell in the back seat. I reached under the seat to adjust it and Denise yelled, "I hope you two bitches got a good high because you sure are wasting enough of my time. Now either kill me or let me go because I don't give a fuck anymore."

I'm so high, I feel like I'm floating and for the moment nothing she said bothered me. "Denise, ain't nobody gonna hurt you." I smiled. "You good. Plus your husband gonna come through. I just know it."

"Yeah, just relax," Crystal said slapping her on the shoulder. Her eyes were glassy and red and I wondered what mine looked like. "You keep being cool and I have a feeling we gonna let you go."

We tried to reach Hollywood several times again but nothing happened. Maybe he was on the plane headed back to Atlanta. I decided that we would drive around so nobody would stop us and ask us any questions. So for the next forty minutes I drove in silence, with no special place to go.

"I'm hungry, bitch, you hear me?" Denise said all of a sudden.

When I looked at her she was staring in my direction. "What you just say to me?" I scratched my head.

"You heard me, bitch! I said I'm hungry. Pull over and let me get something to eat. You might as well."

"First off if you call me *bitch* one more time I'ma push you out this car while I'm driving."

"And here I thought you were the nice one," she said to me. "But I knew you would reveal your true personality sooner or later."

"I'm warning you to shut the fuck up," I yelled at her again. Usually the weed calmed me down but for some reason I was agitated.

"'Bout time you gave it to this bitch," Crystal said closing her eyes. "She been getting on my nerves all night."

"Like I said, either take me to get something to eat or I'm gonna make this ride uncomfortable by screaming my face off," Denise threatened.

"And how do you plan on doing that?" Crystal said. "You not in no position to be—"

She screamed so loud my eardrums rattled. "Aight, aight, calm the fuck down!" I yelled. "I'm gonna let you grab something now." I quickly turned into some country fried chicken joint, which was the first place I saw. Besides, after smoking I'm kind of hungry too. I pulled up in a secluded area of the parking lot behind the restaurant, near the dumpster.

"What the fuck you want?" I asked parking. "And don't be ordering too much because until your husband do what he gotta, funds are limited." I lied, as if we didn't have the other money in the trunk.

"Give me a fried chicken sandwich, Tasha," Crystal interrupted.

I shook my head. "You have zero manners."

I took Denise's order, which was some chicken strips and a diet soda. I got out of the car, and I walked around the building and inside where there was a long line. Irritated, I'm in the restaurant for fifteen minutes before my food finally comes out.

When I come back to the car I see Denise holding a gun to my sister's face. From the window Denise is grinning at me and my sister looks horrified. Like she knows her life is about to be over. *No. No. No. No. No.* I said to myself. *This can't be happening.*

As I looked at her I felt helpless.

I walked up to the window. "What you doing?" I asked her.

"Get in the car and untie my legs and other arm," Denise demanded. "Or I'ma blow this bitch's face off."

Instead of doing what she asked I dropped the bag of food on the ground; opened the car door, released the gun from my waist that I stole from Crystal out the backseat and fire into the car window. Shooting Denise in the face.

LEVEL UP

Wow, now I had to add murder to the list of things I'd done wrong. Fuck!

CHAPTER TWELVE
HOLLYWOOD

*M*onique Burton was exhausted and didn't feel like going to her doctor's appointment later but still she had to. She was not allowed to drive but neither Tasha nor Crystal had bothered to call and tell her who was taking her.

Her mind was a living nightmare. Thoughts floated around always and if she wasn't consumed with ideas that someone was out to get her, she was consumed with thinking about her daughters and how awful a mother she'd been throughout the years. It was a living hell.

Initially Monique pretended like she didn't remember her daughter's crazy childhood whenever Crystal wanted to speak about it, but she recalled everything. During the worst time in Monique's life she ran with a gang. Although they sold drugs their real hustle was murder for hire and anybody could get it. At first Monique, with her beauty and wild spirit, assisted the gang by luring men to their deaths, with promises of sex. But when word got out that she was scandalous she needed to find another way and that's where her girls came in.

Luring strangers by claiming to give sexual acts from full sex to blowjobs, Tasha and Crystal would lead dealers or rich men away from their homes and cars only to be kidnapped and held for ransom. Because of their beauty over twenty men had met their deaths with their assistance. And although Monique tried to put those days out of her mind, Crystal never got over the past and feared one of the victims' family members would soon find and kill them. This was one of the reasons Monique believed both of her daughters were gay. Believing that seeing how low dirty men would stoop to have sex with young girls disgusted them.

Monique sat Lil' Kevin on the sofa and ate her tuna fish sandwich when she heard a knock at the door. Expecting one of her daughters she opened it wearing her red housecoat. "Who you?" She asked the attractive man standing before her. "And what you doing at my house?"

"What's up, sexy?" He extended his hand. "My name is Hollywood and this is my driver Doc." Doc nodded and smiled.

Monique clutched the collar of her robe to be sure she was not naked. "If you calling me sexy either you blind or stupid. Now do me a favor and tell me which one it is?" She waited.

"I know what I said and I'm talking about you," He responded. "I think you are a very appealing woman."

Monique looked behind her.

"May I come in? We come bearing gifts." Hollywood looked behind him at his driver who raised a grocery bag.

"Well why didn't you say so?" With that fake offer. Monique backed up and allowed the killers into her home. Once the door was closed Hollywood walked up to the sofa and looked down at the dog who was tearing into the sandwich.

"What breed is it?" Hollywood asked.

"I don't know," Monique shrugged. "I just call it a dog."

He smiled. "Well what's its name?"

LEVEL UP

"Lil' Kevin," she responded, wondering what he wanted. "Now what do you really need from me? You're acting too strange for my taste."

Hollywood turned around and faced her. "Like I said we brought groceries for you and your family. What did we get again, Doc?"

"Steaks, shrimp, chops. And some dessert too."

"That's right...steak and shrimp," he repeated nodding slowly. "You do eat steak in this house don't you?"

"If it had a heart beat we fries it up around here," Monique responded as she eyed him closer. Something didn't feel right.

"That's good to hear," Hollywood chuckled. "Now, are you the lady of the house?" From where he stood he looked around.

"I am," she nodded.

"Great, because I've been trying desperately to reach Crystal and Tasha. You see, we go way back and it's been such a long time since I've seen them." He snapped his finger and pointed at her. "I know Crystal had a birthday a month ago," he continued, remembering the pictures he saw on her social media page. "And I was unable to go to the party since I was out of town. It was family business and all. So I figured I'd come today and cook for her."

"Oh, is that right?" Monique responded as the dog continued to bark crazily. "Well it wasn't that big of a party. Just a few friends and stuff."

He nodded. "Yeah, I still wanted to be there but you know how life gets in the way."

"A lot of things get in the way to be honest." She smiled. "But you have to live as long as me to know that."

Hollywood laughed and then suddenly with a straight face he said, "Your daughters...do you know where they are? I need to see them right away."

Before she could respond Tiffani rushed inside of the house talking on the phone. She looked like a young man.

"Bitch, them Jays Leila be selling fake as fuck and I told her. So she got mad and said she was gonna fight me when she saw me but I'm waiting." She paused and stood in the middle of the living room looking at Hollywood, Doc and Monique. "I'm at my girl's house now but maybe we can get together later. Since Crystal being trifling and not answering my calls." She looked at their serious faces. "But let me hit you back." She dropped the phone in her pocket and crossed her arms over her chest. "What's up, Ms. M?" She looked at the men. "I ain't know you were having company. I remember Crystal saying you needed a ride to the doctors so I'm here."

"We got company." Monique said. "They aren't here for me. They here for the girls."

Tiffani looked Hollywood and Doc over. "Who you?"

"I'm Hollywood and we trying to find Tasha and Crystal, do you know where they are?"

"Well I don't know where Crystal's cheating ass is but if you looking for Tasha you need to visit her girlfriend. She's always at her crib."

Hollywood looked at Doc slyly and then back at Tiffani. "You can help us with that right?"

"Shit, for fifty dollars I'll tell you whatever you need." She shrugged. "Ya'll friends right?"

Hollywood and Doc nodded slyly.

CHAPTER THIRTEEN
CRYSTAL

The air was thick and muggy inside *Trap Girl's Strip Club*. I was on my way to the back, to get away from the crowd and ease into the VIP. Once there I was sitting on a chair in a private room and Sunshine was on her knees, between my legs eating my pussy. Whenever we stopped here to sell the things we robbed from the houses to the club owner, I would make it my mission to hook up with Sunshine. She didn't play when it came to her head game and because of it she was my favorite.

Normally I don't go this hard. With doing stuff like this out in the open. But whenever I was stressed it helped me get shit off my mind. I really needed this after watching my sister kill that bitch in front of me and it fucked up my head. Before Tasha even pulled the trigger I could tell by looking in her eyes that she was forever changed behind that move and I can't help but blame myself.

All she wanted was to run away with her girl and I had different ideas. And now look? We were both walking dead bitches. It was like I knew I could be selfish but there was no way I could stop myself.

"You tasting real sweet tonight," Sunshine said looking up at me. "I love when you come see me. You so fucking sexy." They called her Sunshine because of a skit she does when she dances. While on the pole she'll open up her legs where a flash bulb is stuck in her coochie and shines out. It was a hit with the niggas but I love her lick game more.

Feeling good, I looked down at her, while grabbing the back of her long red hair. "Why you talking instead of licking?" I asked, biting my bottom lip. "Get back to work."

She looked up at me. "Just wanted you to know," — she shrugged — "Sometimes when you come in here I get sad because I thought you really liked me. You broke up with your girl yet? I heard she almost got into a fight with Leila earlier in—"

"Just eat my pussy, Sunshine." I paused looking at her sternly. "I ain't come in here for all that other shit."

She looked at my shirt. "Hold up, why you got blood on you?" She touched it. "You hurt or something?"

"Just focus on your job, Sunshine unless you don't want this money." I frowned, slapping her hand away. "I could give it to someone else."

As she went back to work I could see my sister through a small window on the door. She was in the front of the club, trying to buy some ID's and passports so we could run away and get out of town. We had enough money to last a little while but I could tell this situation was making her stressed. Besides, she would be running away with ma and me. And not Nikki.

When Sunshine ran her tongue around my clit I think I thought I was about to cum. Especially when she started flipping it quick. "Don't forget to lick the tunnel."

"But you never could handle it when I did that," she giggled. "I will though if you come back more."

I frowned. She was really trying to blow me. "See this the dumb shit that makes me wonder why I fuck with you anyway."

"Damn, Crystal, I'm just playing with you." She rolled her eyes. "I mean why you getting all stupid and shit?"

"Stupid?" I pushed her off. "You know what, get the fuck up."

"No…no…don't, don't go, please." She paused and I stood up. "I need the money and I know you ain't cum yet. You know I be talking shit because you set me off and I like you. I ain't mean nothing really. I just want to make sure that you one hundred percent good." I was still frowning at her. "Please don't go. You got me on my knees begging."

I glared. "Then do less yapping and more licking." I coached. "Plus I got somewhere else to be." I sat back down.

"For you to be so feminine you so mean." She grinned. "But for some reason I like that shit."

"What did I just say?" This girl was gonna make me slap the fuck out of her.

She smiled and started lapping again. I was pawning the back of her head when I saw the club owner hand my sister something. When Tasha put it away, she looked toward the back of the club and squinted at the VIP room. I know she was trying to see if I was inside and I think she spotted me.

Aw shit, this bitch is about to start tripping.

Tasha rushed up to the VIP room, flung the door open and looked down at Sunshine and back at me. "I know you not dumb enough to be back here getting your pussy ate when we got business in the car." She was referring to Denise's body, which for now was stuffed in her trunk. "Sweetheart, get your shit up and get the fuck out of here." She said to Sunshine. "My sister done for the day." She threw her a fifty-dollar bill and Sunshine snatched it up and ran out.

I pulled up my jeans and zipped them up. Then I dusted the back of my fat ass in case I sat on something. "Why you do that? She ain't even make me bust yet!"

She pointed in my face. "Crystal, you that fucking gone in the head that you don't realize what's popping off right now? What's wrong with you? I think you bipolar too. Like ma."

"Did you get the money from the stuff or not? 'Cause I'm tired of all this—"

I'm caught off guard by the blow I just took to the face, courtesy of my sister. As a matter of fact I couldn't remember the last time she hit me. But if I had to pin point a time it may have been when I snuck her phone away after she broke up with Nikki last year to stop her from going crazy.

We were drinking at this club and to help her mind off Nikki I took it. Not to be petty but I figured if she didn't have her phone she couldn't wait for her to call. But instead of telling her I had it, I convinced her that

LEVEL UP

she lost it at the club and she was too drunk to dispute. The truth was once we got home I pushed it to the bottom of my dog's bed thinking that would be it for a while.

Everyday she would call and check the voicemails but would be too late because I erased all Nikki's messages. After awhile she thought Nikki hadn't called and moved on which was my plan all along. I even went as far as to delete the message on the house phone too.

Tasha looked like death walking around the house, not eating or talking to anybody. But after awhile she came to terms that it was over or at least I thought so. We were outside drinking when she said, "I'm gonna ask her to marry me."

I begged her not to but she whipped a ring out her pocket to show me she was serious. That's when I had to come clean, knowing that Nikki would tell her that she'd been calling non-stop.

When she was in her room later that night I knocked on the door and handed her the cell phone. At first she was relieved to have it back, especially after I told her Nikki called, but a second later she was the angriest I'd ever seen. She got up from the bed, stepped in front of me and hit me like I was a nigga. My tooth loosened in my mouth and everything.

But tonight I'm tired of her. So I rubbed my jaw and delivered a blow so hard to her stomach that her mouth spread open and spit flew out. Oh well, I guess we 'bout to fight it out now.

CHAPTER FOURTEEN
TASHA

"Ya'll gotta get out of here with this shit," somebody said behind me, as I gut punched Crystal over and over. She may have been smaller than me but she was strong as fuck and needed a few blows to go down. I know this is wrong but at this moment she not my sister. For real I got more love for a nigga on the street than I do for her right now. I just killed somebody on a count of her having *another* gun that she purchased from Asian Lucy the other night without telling me. I remembered her talking to her that night on a side convo but I had no idea she was buying a weapon until this situation with Denise.

If you asked me she probably been planning on robbing Hollywood for the longest and I'm just finding out now. I'm done with my sister and tired of her selfish shit.

"I can't have this in my establishment," Keith said looking between us. "So the both of you have to go outside and cool off or you won't be allowed back in here. Ever. Even for those documents you need." He looked at me.

I didn't respond. Instead I slapped Crystal one more time sending her flying onto the dirty floor. When she got up she tried to hit me back but I shoved her into the bouncer who walked up behind us.

"That's it, I'm sorry, Tasha, but I can't have this shit in my club," Keith said firmly. He looked at the bouncer. "Aye, Joe launch these two out for awhile. Hopefully they'll cool off."

I don't know how he did it but Joe managed to lift us off of our feet, before tossing us out into the front of the club. But it doesn't stop us from goin' at each other once more.

We shoving and pushing each other until Crystal finally said, "Why you leaving?" Leaning on her knees she said, "Why you wanna walk out on me like this?"

"Fuck you talking 'bout now?" I shoved her again and she slammed into a black BMW. "Why do you keep asking me the same things repeatedly?" I wiped the sweat off my face. "Anyway, I'm not trying to hear none of that right now. I'm tired of your recklessness, Crystal." I pointed at her. "I can truly say that I'm done."

"Am I that bad?" She asked ignoring my questions. "Am I that awful that you would want to leave me forever?"

I'm breathing heavily as I throw myself on the curb next to the car Crystal is leaning on. "It's not my responsibility to take care of you no more." I rubbed the knot I felt popping up on my forehead and looked up at her. "My leaving don't have nothing to do with you. I told you that a million times and I don't understand why you don't get it." I paused. "I'm just in love."

"Then why it feel like it's my fault? We had plans for the future and now I feel like nothing I say will convince you not to go."

"Because it won't. I don't know what else to say, Crystal," I shook my head slowly. "What I suggest is this though…you gotta stop fucking these nasty ass bitches out here. Getting burned and all that. As pretty as you are you in the back getting top from a skank like a nigga." I paused. "I got a girl, Crystal. Can't you understand that shit? This is making me crazy because I keep telling you the same thing."

"I do have someone."

"But you don't care about her like I care about mine." I paused. "So you can't compare the two."

"Man this is off plan." She ran her hand down her face. "Way off and nothing good is gonna come of this."

I shook my head. "Why you asking me this now?"

"Because I feel that I'm about to lose you forever."

I stood up. I'm still mad so it's hard for me to look her directly in the eyes. "Crystal, you gotta know that no matter what happens you'll always have me in your life. But we adults now and we gotta go after our own dreams. It don't mean you'll lose me though. But the

LEVEL UP

shit you doing these days making me feel like you don't give a fuck 'bout nobody but yourself."

"I fucked up didn't I?"

I looked around and stepped closer so that only she could hear my words. "We got a woman in the trunk of a car, Crystal," I whispered. "The wife of a well known trap nigga who knows who we are. You can't get more fucked up than this if you tried." I backed up a little. "I actually killed somebody tonight. And you have no idea all the thoughts I got goin' on in my mind right now. The guilt alone is enough to put me into panic mode. But that's not goin' to help anything so I gotta be strong for me and you. But I'll never be happy again when this shit is over, Crystal. I'll never feel safe either." I pointed at her. "And I got you to blame for this shit."

She lowered her head and I could see tears roll down her face until her hair fell alongside her jawline. "This is so crazy."

I tried to touch her to give her a hug. "Just get the fuck off me!" She paused. "Don't put your fucking hands on me period."

I raised my hands in the air and backed up. "What's wrong with you now? I thought we was talking."

"It don't even matter." She wiped her tears away. "Let's just go because I gotta get out of here."

Inside The Club

Keith, the club's owner, was on the phone behind the bar looking at Tasha and Crystal outside of the club acting like kids. Although the music was loud, it wasn't stopping him from doing what he was about to do. Snitch. "Hey, man, ain't you looking for the Burton girls?"

"You know the answer to that already," Hollywood said on the other end of the phone. "So you telling me something I wanna hear or are you wasting my time?"

LEVEL UP

"They down here. At my club."

There was a moment of long silence. "If you can keep them there I got ten large waiting for you." He paused. "That's a promise."

"Fuck," he paused. "I should've hit you first."

"What you saying?"

"I threw them out a minute ago but with that kinda pay day on the table, trust me, I'll think of something."

"Good, because I'm sending somebody right now to collect them bitches."

CHAPTER FIFTEEN
CRYSTAL

Hot water flowed down on Tiffani's dreads as she stood under the showerhead at the house. After we left the club and stashed the car with the body for the moment, I took our car and my half of the money and decided to go to Tiff's, while Tasha took an Uber to God knows where. Keith was trying to get us to stay around, even offered us free drinks, but that made Tasha extra nervous so we didn't stay.

I never thought I'd see the day but after our conversation was over it became clear that Tasha and I were no longer sisters. And at the end of the day I gotta be cool with that whether I wanted to or not.

I'm watching Tiff ring out her dreads and for some reason it turned me on. So I pushed the shower curtain back and said, "Get out, Tiff, and come to bed. I'm ready."

She grinned. "You must want me to fuck the dog shit out of you again." She smiled. "I know that look in your eyes anywhere."

"If by that you mean eat this pussy the answer is yes." I smiled. "Now come on and hurry up."

She turned the water off and stepped out of the tub, leaving a water trail behind her. Tying her dreads up she bopped over to me where I was sitting and waiting. Tiffani was dominant but she also had a soft appeal that did something to me. I cared about her. But enough to do forever? I couldn't be sure.

Before she made it to the bed I changed my mind. "As a matter of fact," I paused. "Drop to the floor." I opened my legs wide. "And assume the position."

"Somebody extra horny," she said flipping her loose dreads out the way. "You fighting with your sister again or something? That's the only time you be like this."

I rolled my eyes. "Nah, I just want you to lick it," I told her. "Now stop playing around and lets do this."

She crawled over to me and her dreads fell out the towel. "You don't have to tell me twice, sexy."

I slid my finger into my pussy and she pushed my legs further apart. After flipping my clit five or six times she slipped her tongue along the side of it, before rolling it to the other side. I took a shower earlier because if Tiffani can smell anything it's the scent of another bitch, even if I didn't rub myself on her. I didn't want her tripping off Sunshine when we weren't even a thing. Besides, I didn't get a chance to cum thanks to my hating ass sister anyway.

"Make it wet, Tiff," I said looking down at her biting my lip. "You know how I like it so do it just like that."

"Aye, Crystal, don't come at me like I don't know how to satisfy you. I just had you crawling up the bedpost earlier, which is why I don't understand why you still horny." She placed her hands on my legs again. "Keep it real, I'm the only bitch who can make you cum in under two."

Tiff's telling the truth but I always like to challenge her. "Maybe back in the day but lately I think you falling off, Tiff." I lied. "It's been taking you longer than usual to get me there."

"Oh yeah?" One minute I'm sitting on the bed and the next she has lifted me up. My pussy is in her face as she's walking around the room going to work. You had to be strong to do that and she was. "Shit, Tiffani," I said. "Fuck you doing?"

She didn't respond. Instead she sunk her tongue into the center of my pussy and sucked so hard my clit trembled. Spit drizzled and oozed down her chin and my eyes rolled to the back of my head. It wasn't long before my pussy tingled and pulsated. "Damn, damn, Tiffani," I moaned. "Hold up a minute. You gonna make me cum too quick."

She doesn't stop, instead she continued to slurp and suck on my pussy until it felt so good I wanted to cry. I was done. There's nothing I can do but go along for the ride. Instead of fighting I pawned the back of her head and pushed into her face.

"You bet not drop me bitch," I said before she flipped her tongue again. "Awwww shit, fuck," I moaned.

Tiffani didn't stop until all my cream spilled over her face. When she was done she placed me down on the bed. "In case you were wondering," she pointed at the clock. "That took one minute and forty seconds. So don't fuck with me when it comes to my head game."

When my mind flashed on Hollywood's wife for some reason I got horny again. Not because death turned me on but because I want to get it out my mind. "Lay down. I'm not done yet."

She picked up the towel off the floor that she used to dry her dreads and tossed it on the chair. Folding her arms in front of me she said, "So you want me on the bed too? You haven't had enough yet?"

"No, I'm not done." She eased on the bed. I crawled on top of her and mounted her pussy. With my pussy still juicy I slid all over hers while kissing the side of her neck. She winded her waist and pulled me down closer making my clit feel like it was sliding over a little hump. Every time she did that motion my pussy tingled more.

"Move that shit, Crystal!" She said guiding my motions. "I'ma fuck the shit out of your pretty ass!"

"I see you talking shit." I raised my head and kissed her lips. "You better keep moving that pussy though. This feeling way too good."

"You already know what it is," she said. "It ain't like you don't know how I get down."

In the past I have been known to hold back on talking sexually to Tiffani when I'm fucking her in the bedroom. There was a reason though. One time I said one thing too many and we got into a fight after I said another woman's name. But she seemed like she all in tonight so I might as well go with it.

"What you waiting on?" I asked. "Fuck me."

Suddenly she pushed up into me while pulling me down harder. I could feel her clit getting stiffer. When I looked down her eyes were closed and the bed beneath us was wetter which meant at any moment she was about to cum.

"Now talk that shit, bitch." I said, moving in circular motions.

"Just keep it right there, Crystal," she begged. "Just, just don't move." She continued to guide my hips. "Just don't go anywhere." She paused. "Damn," she said as she pulled me so hard she scratched the side of my meaty ass. "Fuck!" She said letting me go. "That was, so fucking good."

I rolled off her and looked up at the ceiling. My breath quick and heavy. "Yeah, it was. I needed that too."

She looked over at me. "Crystal…what's on your mind?"

"Nothing."

"That was back to back fucking." She stared. "Since when have we gone there?"

"What you thought it was a game, Tiff?" I laughed. "You thought I was playing when I said I wanted to fuck all night?"

"Crystal, I enjoy making love to you but you been real weird lately." She touched my hand. "And I wanna tell you something else too."

I rolled on my side so that I could fully look at her. "What is it?"

"I don't think I can be with you." She flipped her wet dreads out of her face.

My eyes widened. "Why? I thought we were chilling just now. Fuck I do this time?"

She sat up. "I don't trust you."

"Why?" I paused. "Just because I got a lot—"

"That ain't no excuse, Crystal. You can't keep saying you got a lot on your mind and still cheat and shit."

By NIKKI. K

"Cheat?"

"I know 'bout the girl Sunshine."

I stood up, grabbed a few pieces of tissue out the dispenser, wiped myself and slipped into my tight jeans in case we had to fight. "What you talking about? I don't even know who that is."

"My friend saw you in VIP." She paused, and cracked her knuckles. "So instead of fighting you it's over."

"So you would fuck me and then break up with me just like that?" I looked over at her. "People say I'm cold but you just took the cake."

"You do shit like this all the time." She said. "Plus I wanted you to remember how good it was."

I walked up to the bed and sat down on the edge. Placing my face in my hands I said, "Please don't do this right now. If ever you picked a wrong time now is it."

She sat on the bed with her back against the headboard. "Wow," she paused, wiping her dreads over her shoulder. "I thought you wouldn't give a fuck anymore."

"I do and I know shit been fucked up but with my sister leaving I can't let you go too." I took a deep breath and tried to think about why this was happening. Why my life was crumbling down. Tasha always said if I didn't stop being so selfish I would lose everyone I loved. Now I was starting to believe she was right.

"Crystal, if you really want to be in a relationship with me you have to talk to me." She paused. "Because I'm serious about walking away this time. I finally realize I can be by myself."

I wiped my long hair out of my face and looked at her. I wanted to tell her about the robberies, the murder and everything else, but Tiff has a big mouth and might start telling everybody before I got a chance to correct the problem. "It's about this nigga named Hollywood."

"Wait," she sat up and looked over at me. "You talking about the dude who came to your house earlier today?" She snapped her finger like she was trying to remember something else. "The one who looks like a drug dealer?"

I leaned closer. "What, what did you just say?"

"Some dude was at your house today. Your mother said he was a friend. He even took your moms to her doctor's appointment and everything. He seemed nice and I thought he was cool. Why? Something wrong?"

I stood up and started pacing. "Are you saying to me that this man was in my house and that he has my mother?" I paused. "And you just telling me this now? After we've been together all this time?"

"What?" She shrugged. "He ain't your friend? Because that's what he said when I came in. He was already there and everything." She shrugged again. "Brought food and some more shit."

"Tiff, why wouldn't you tell me when I came over earlier?" I placed my hand over my heart. Trying to stop the thunder. "We stopped by the store and everything! At no point did you think to tell me that he had my mother?"

"My bad, Crystal." She stood up and walked in front of me. "I mean, did I do something wrong? I'm telling you it didn't seem that serious when I was there. That's why I didn't tell you." She shrugged again. "So I guess I'm telling you now."

CHAPTER SIXTEEN
TASHA

I was lying in Carmen's bed and she was on top of me. We just finished fucking and I wanted her to get up so I could think about my next moves. But she's big on cuddling after sex and does this all the time. It's her way of trying to never let me go.

Carmen is a cute short redbone with long black hair. She's exactly the opposite of Nikki and I like it that way because it gives me variety. Back in the day I was only attracted to dark skin girls with big asses and small facial features like Nikki. But as I got older it became all about the conversation and who gives me less drama.

After me and my sister got into it earlier tonight I could've called Nikki and went over her house, since she lives alone, but she asked too many questions. Plus I don't feel like talking about my sister right now and that's all she wants to do. Use our fights to bash her.

For the most part Carmen is easy goin', although she has a sneaky side too that I haven't figured out yet. I been dealing with her off and on for months now and never had a major problem because she seemed low-key.

"What's on your mind, Tasha?" She asked. "Because you look like you somewhere else when you need to be here." She paused. "Plus I'm tired of having to compete for your attention."

I squeezed her ass cheeks and she fingered my short curly hair. "What you need to be asking is what's up with that pussy." I slapped her ass. "Because right now it's a little tart and needs to be washed."

She giggled. "You so fucking nasty," she said hitting my arm. "I'm serious though. You look like you got a lot on your mind. You and Nikki didn't get into it again did you? I saw how upset she was when she came to my house the other night and saw you here. The last thing I want is for ya'll to be fighting over me. That's why I stayed inside."

"What I tell you about saying Nikki's name?" I frowned. "Didn't I tell you I don't want you talking about her? Period. What we do is what we do and it's as simple as that."

"Damn, Tasha, you acting like I'm gonna call her up or something." She waved the air. "Ain't nobody thinking nothing about your little girlfriend. Trust me, it's not that deep on my side. And keep all that extra emotional shit out my house please."

She talking real slick now. Which is something she normally didn't do. "You know what…just get off me." She placed her hand flat on my chest and pushed off of me. "You a stupid bitch."

"You the stupid bitch," she said pointing at me. "I'm done with you. And don't ever come back here again." Her eyes were all wide and crazy. "I'm serious this time, Tasha. I'm done with the back and forth shit. We really over now."

I stomped out and walked to the bathroom to grab my clothes because we started having sex in there and worked our way to her room. When I'm done I go back into her bedroom and she's staring at me. "I'm leaving." I told her getting dressed. "Let me just put my stuff on."

"I know you leaving because I want you gone anyway." She paused. "I don't know why you trying to pretend like you doing something I don't want."

I laughed. Is every woman in my life crazy? Maybe I attract this type of dysfunction and didn't realize it. Maybe I have to change everything about my energy or something…Nah, it's definitely these bitches. "Like I said, I'm gone. And your pussy dead anyway."

"My pussy dead?" She repeated walking up to me. "Bitch, is that why you be beating down the interstate to get at this shit? Because it's dead? I doubt that very seriously, ma'am, thanks for the lies anyway though. Because if anybody's pussy dead it's yours."

As she screamed and ranted I felt a little guilty. This wasn't her at all and I knew it. She had to be picking up on my bad vibes. Although I'm not feeling her the real reason my mind is gone has nothing to do with her. I guess it's like transference of energy.

When I first got over here I took a nap because I was too stressed to stay awake. Apparently I was having a nightmare that my girl was murdered and started screaming in my sleep. When I woke up Carmen was next to me, pushing me, and trying to wake me up. Part of me felt bad because if something happened to Nikki while I was in this bed it would crush me.

With all that said no matter what I got goin' on in my life Carmen had been drama free and I owed her more than this. She never gave me trouble and minded her tongue when Nikki called. And although I'm sure it will be my last time coming over here, I didn't want to bounce on bad terms.

"...so you don't ever have to worry about me again, Tasha." She had been talking the entire time and I tuned her out. Something I learned to do with Nikki and Crystal.

Running my hand down my face I took a deep breath. I had to stop leaving hurt people in my wake, especially since there was a possibility if I couldn't get the passports that I would get killed.

Originally I was going to use Keith to get our documents but he gave me the creeps when we were in his establishment. At first he wanted us gone because we were bad for business when Crystal and I got into a fight. But right when we were about to leave he came outside, and tried to get us to come back in. I'm not sure but I believe he was working with Hollywood. "Look, Carmen, I'm sorry," I said to her. "I'm taking shit out on you."

"What?" She folded her arms over her breasts. "You...you're sorry?"

"Yes." I grabbed both her hands. "Listen...some shit went down tonight and I've been mad in the head. It don't give you the right to come at me like you did either," I pointed at her. "But I can understand why you would be mad though."

She smiled. "Girl, you were trying to give me a heart attack with the way you were talking. I'm not use to having bitches disrespect like that. Getting me all in my feelings for nothing."

"You right and I'm never gonna come at you like that again but I do gotta bounce though." I paused. "There's some stuff with my sister that I gotta clear up."

"I understand, bae, do what you gotta do." She smiled and wiped her hand down my cheek. "Its not that heavy with me. Whenever you ready I'll be here." She winked. "The invitation is open again now by the way."

"I got you, ma," I replied knowing I was never coming back. I had to get out of this country. My days of staying in Atlanta were over. "I'll let you know when I have some more time."

I threw the rest of my clothes on and slipped into my sneakers. When my wallet fell off the table on the side of the bed I picked it up. When I saw a pill bottle I snatched it. I don't know what made me look at it but something about it stood out to me.

When I zeroed in on the label closely I saw it was an antibiotic. I gripped it in my hand and walked over to her. "Fuck is this, Carmen? Are you, are you burning?"

"What, what you talking about now, Tasha?" She backed away a little. "You know I'm not burning. Don't be stupid."

I extended my hand so that it was up in her face. "Then what the fuck is this?" She paused. "If you not burning what is it?"

She immediately started crying. "I'm sorry, Tasha. When you called and said you were coming over at first I wasn't going to have sex with you. Because I knew about my condition. But then you were so sad that I did it out of pity."

I glared. "Out of pity?" I could feel my heart thumping in my chest. "Fuck you talking about, bitch? I don't need nobody to pity me! And give me a disease. Fuck is wrong with you?"

"I'm serious." She said extending her hands in my direction. "I was in this house all by myself and I was lonely. So I...so I said it wouldn't be bad when you wanted to come over because you sounded sad."

"What do you have, Carmen?" I took several deep breaths. "I'm not fucking around. Tell me right now before I unleash in here."

"Nothing really. It's only—"

"What the fuck you got?" I yelled again.

"Syphilis." She folded her arms again and rubbed them. "Okay? Are you satisfied? And ain't no need in you losing your mind. It should be all cleared up now."

My eyes widened and the pill bottle fell out my hand. This bitch is crazy. Who does some vile shit like fuck somebody while sick? "You made me eat your pussy when you burning?"

"It's cleared up now, Tasha!" She yelled. "I only have a few more pills to take and I'm done. I don't know what else you want me to say."

I stared at her hard. I wanted to smack the syphilis out this bitch!

"You know what, fuck all this shit." She said putting her hands on her hips. "It ain't like your sister didn't give it to me anyway. If anything you should be going off on her. Not me."

My jaw hung. "Hold up, you fucked my, my sister?"

"Every chance I get." I guess she was done playing the victim because her response was snooty.

Irritated, I slapped her to the floor and pointed down at her face. "You dead to me, whore." I paused. "And you better hope I don't get five extra minutes because I'ma come back over here and fuck you up."

She stood up and held her face. "We'll see about that," she smiled.

I was so mad I stomped down the steps of her house. And the moment I pushed the front door open I saw my sister approaching. Once again she got some dumb shit going on by fucking my number two for no reason.

Still, what she doing over here now?

CHAPTER SEVENTEEN
HOLLYWOOD

Hollywood walked downstairs in the basement of the car dealership he owned, with Doc following his every step in protection mode. Ms. Burton sat tied up on a metal chair and her mouth was duct taped.

Behind Hollywood were four of his men who were waiting on orders on what Hollywood's next wish would be. Ms. Burton was visibly shaken and afraid and it made a lot of sense. For starters she didn't know what was happening and why. Every so often she would look around, waiting for the next vile move but as of yet nothing happened.

"Has either of them bitches called yet," Hollywood asked one of his men. "This shit is taking longer than I wanted."

"No, we been sitting by the phone though," one man responded. "We on full charge too." He raised his cell phone.

"Well this doesn't make much sense," Hollywood said looking down at her. "Why wouldn't they call for their own mother?" He observed Monique's shivering body. "Do your children fuck with you?" He asked although he needed no response. In his opinion it was evident by their actions.

"Don't hurt me, young man," she mumbled through tape. "Please. You don't have to do this."

"They're probably waiting to see if you'll give them the money they asking for first," Doc said.

"Yeah, before they return your wife," another responded.

"Nah, they probably don't think I'll hurt her," Hollywood responded. "If they do feel that way they don't know me very well." He paused. "Check that phone again, Doc. Is it on?"

"Yep," he raised the phone in the air for the fifth time for the evening. It was like Hollywood was stalling on making a move. "I got full signal strength and everything. Still no call though."

Hollywood looked down and ran his hand down his face. He hated himself for never considering the angle that his wife could be kidnapped, let alone by two women. In his mind people weren't idiotic enough to fuck with her but he was wrong. In the pursuit of money some would rob anybody.

"You know what, find that chick," Hollywood demanded.

"Who, sir?" Dock asked.

"The one I left alive to give the message who obviously did not because there is no word on my wife." He paused. "Had I known they didn't care about their mother I would've snatched that dyke bitch instead."

"I'll find out where the aggressive female is, sir." Doc said, referring to Tiffani. Before leaving he walked over to Hollywood and whispered into his ear.

"Oh yeah, go back to that Nikki girl's house too. The one the dyke said is dating Tasha. As a matter of fact bring me both of them. With both I'm sure they'll be willing to hand over my wife then." Hollywood turned to walk up the stairs.

"But, sir," the soldier said. "What do we do about their mother in the meantime?"

"You know what, kill that bitch." He shrugged. "I'm not running a babysitting service."

CHAPTER EIGHTEEN

TASHA

I knew Crystal had something to tell me while we sat in the car. She was behind the steering wheel and I was in the passenger's seat, irritated as fuck. I could tell by the look on her face that something was on her mind and suddenly I forgot all about stepping to her about Carmen. I just wished she got it over with.

"So, so how did things go upstairs?" She asked pointing at the window. "To be honest I thought you stopped fucking her. Didn't know you still had feelings."

I shook my head and laughed. "Wow, wow, wow." I paused. "This keeps getting worse and worse."

"What's so funny?" She continued, wiping her hair behind her ear.

"I know 'bout Carmen, Crystal." I paused. "As sick as it is I know 'bout everything."

Her eyes widened and she leaned back and crossed her arms over her chest. "What, what you talking about?"

"Stop fucking around and be honest for real!" I yelled. "You lie so much that even when you have an in to tell the truth you can't do it. This is why I know you have the same thing ma has. Bipolar disorder."

She looked down at her fingers. Taking a deep breath she said, "It was only one time."

I shook my head and laughed. "First off I know that's a lie too. Second of all I was wrong about that shit on your pussy. Based on what Carmen said you probably have syphilis. And even though it won't matter because Hollywood gonna kill everybody, you better go get that shit checked out as soon as possible." I paused and took a deep breath. "Now I know you didn't come all the way down here to talk to me about my slide."

"Syphilis?" She said to herself. Crystal shook her head and took a deep breath. "I want you to know that this shit, all of it, is my fault." She paused. "And I know you know that already but I wanted you to hear it from me too. And I wish I could take back everything but we don't live in that kind of world."

"Crystal, please tell me something I don't know already." I paused. "Like what do you really want?"

"I am, I just—"

"Crystal, I'm tired of the fucking games! Now stop messing around and tell me what's up. Or I'm about to leave out this car. Don't forget we got a body in a trunk that's goin' to start rotting and stinking any minute."

"Tasha, when I said it was my fault, I mean it's *really* my fault. And before we split up, and you go your separate way, I want you to know everything starting with why I picked Hollywood's house."

My jaw tightened as I embraced for the worst. "Go 'head, Crystal." I crossed my arms over my chest and waited for more shit to make me hate her forever. "I'm listening."

"You know how we run the jobs right?"

"Yeah…we find out who gonna be gone and based on that we break in their houses." I threw my hands up in the air. "So again get to the point."

"Well Hollywood stopping by the post office isn't how I made the decision." She said in a low voice. "I mean, I knew before he came in that I was going to his house. It was just a coincidence."

I dropped my hands at my sides. "What that mean?"

"I knew Denise would be home alone, Tasha." She looked over at me. "I'm telling you I knew she was goin' to be in the house *before* we even went inside. But I wanted us to go anyway."

My eyes widened. I felt like somebody punched me in the stomach, and I could feel my forehead moisten. "Are you, are you saying that when we walked up in the back of that house you knew that bitch was there?" I paused. "And you let me go inside anyway? When you knew I had a future? And you knew I had someone who cared about me at home?"

LEVEL UP

She took a deep breath. "Yes." She ran her hand down her face. "I followed her one day. She was in the mall kissing Hollywood and he gave her a stack of cash. During that time I overheard him saying that he would miss her when he was out of town. Like I said it was a coincidence that he came to stop his mail because she was supposed to be going to meet him the next day wherever he was. And I said fuck it," she shrugged. "I figured we might as well kidnap her and get all the money."

I could feel my temples throb and I clenched my fists. "You ruined my life over what, Crystal? Why did you do this shit to me? Your own sister? Everything you wanted me to get behind I supported one hundred percent, no matter how foul it was. You can't count one day where I haven't been in your corner. And you couldn't be in mine for one moment by leaving me out of this shit?"

"I know." Tears rolled down her face. "And all I can say is that I wasn't thinking. I wanted to know how far you would be willing to go for me, Tasha. I wanted to see if it would be me or Nikki and you chose me.

Even killed that bitch. You might not know it now but since Nikki's been in the picture it hasn't been the same."

As she was talking to me I was thinking that I don't know my sister anymore. I'm thinking that I never knew her ever. And then something else popped in my mind. "You saw me take the gun from the backseat right? Before I went into that chicken spot when Denise said she was hungry?"

"Yes," she nodded.

"You knew, you knew I would kill her." I paused. "Didn't you?"

"Yes."

"But how did you know she had the gun?" I paused. "And how did you know she would provoke me to kill her?"

"I knew because I pulled my other gun on her first." She paused. "I knew she would be mad enough to do just what she did because I untied her arm when she said it hurt."

"But what if she would've fired on you after you let her take it, Crystal?" When I saw a twinkle in her eye I had the answer. "You didn't care because once again it meant more to you to see how far I was willing to go for you."

I thought about stealing her in the jaw but I was tired of fighting her. She'd done so much that I couldn't even think anymore. At the end of the day I knew what kind of person my sister was and I still took the trip. I was just as guilty as her when I thought about it that way. All I know is that I gotta get away from her now. I don't care if I went to jail or not for killing Denise. I will never fuck with my sister again and I put that on God.

"You know I'll never talk to you again right?"

She looked away. "Yes."

I ran my hand down my face again. "Before I leave, I need to ask one last question, Crystal." I paused. "Why you telling me all this now?"

"'Cause Hollywood got ma."

I leaned in and my jaw dropped. "Hollywood got, got what?" I stuttered. "Are you fucking serious?"

"Yes. He came to the house and took ma." She wiped her tears away roughly. "Tiffani told me and I'm letting you know now."

"You wasted all of this fucking time telling me about the dead bitch in the trunk when this nigga got our mother?" I yelled. "Crystal, what…why didn't you lead with that first?"

"I wanted you to know everything before I brought it up, Tasha. Because I'm done lying to you."

"And guess what, it don't make a fucking difference!" I screamed. "Plus you said that shit before. You like a scratched record."

"I know, but I'm being real now."

I sat in the seat and looked into the darkness outside. "When you were a kid I put you before me even when I shouldn't have. You were my kid sister and I wanted to protect you from everything I could. Plus I didn't want you thinking that I would abandon you like dad did us because I knew how important that was to you. To feel secure. But throughout it all you have proved to me that it was and will always be, only about you. Well I'm done. I don't give a fuck what happens to you, even if that nigga puts a bird to your head and squeezes."

"You don't mean that." She said, trying to touch me before I pulled away from her.

"Oh but I do. We not sisters no more, Crystal. I'm out here by myself and you better recognize the same." I paused. "To be honest, I hope that nigga kills you so I can be done with all this shit. I'm out."

"Please talk to me, Tasha!" She cried. "You said as long as I was honest that you would never hurt me." I opened the car door. "Tasha, you don't mean that right?" I got out and slammed the door. "Tasha," she continued to yell from inside the car. "Tasha! What about ma?"

CHAPTER NINETEEN
CRYSTAL

I just watched my sister walk away and now I'm driving the car on the way to Tiff's to smoke and get high. I need to calm down, and get myself together. Plus I had to come up with an idea to get my mother and I couldn't think of one. When I made it to Tiff's house I looked around her neighborhood first to make sure she wasn't on the block. When I didn't see her I jumped out and walked toward her house.

I had to be careful though. Times were dangerous. Plus I didn't know who's watching the house or me walking inside. When I walked into the living room she was inside doing push ups.

"Why you in here acting like ain't nothing wrong?" I asked. "After you were late on the info for my mother? And you know I'm trying to find her. It's like you don't care."

"What do you want, Crystal?" She sighed and I felt bad when I looked at her face. Her eye was swollen and she had a knot on her forehead. When she didn't tell me Hollywood had our mother we got into a big fight. It was the worst fight we'd ever gotten in and I thought the police would get called. In the end we just stopped beefing and I walked out. "Just get out my house. I told you it's over. I mean it this time."

Not paying her any attention I walked in and sat on the sofa and watched her exercise. "Can we talk before I go?" I paused. "It won't take long I promise."

"'Bout what, Crystal?"

I wiped my hair out of my face. "I need some more information on what Hollywood was driving when he came over my mother's house." I paused. "Because he definitely has her against her will. I'm sure of it."

She took a deep breath. "Like I told you before, I was on the phone and didn't pay any attention to any cars on the block." She paused. "If I had I would've told you earlier today. Stop asking me over and over like I'm an idiot."

I looked down at Tiff who had finished one more pushup before she sat on the sofa, arms crossed over her chest. "I hear all that but you had to see something. And if you would take time to think instead of being mad at me you would remember."

"I think something is wrong with you, Crystal." She paused. "You just like your mother. Plus you so used to disrespecting people that you think things are normal." She paused. "I want you out because like I said this time it's over for real."

"You can't be here, Tiff," I looked over at her. "It's not safe. That's also why I came by so put a shirt on, stop looking all crazy and come with me."

"If it's true, and Hollywood is after you because of something you did, then why would I run?" She grabbed the remote and turned on the TV. "They after you not me. Just leave me out all this mess."

"Are you really this stupid or just slow?"

She smiled. "You fought me like a nigga, tried to fuck my friend before I gave you a pass and you ruined my life!" She yelled. "So what part don't you understand when I say it's over?"

I placed my hands over my face and screamed into my palms. "How many times do I have to keep saying I'm sorry? Over the same shit."

"And still its over." She turned around to look at me. "Crystal, I mean if you had a problem with me why did you keep fucking me? If you hated me as much as you do why not just leave me alone?"

"I don't hate you, Tiff."

"Well why Mercy tell me you fucked her again when I left out to make your food that night?" She pointed in my face. "And why did a friend of mine call and tell me you hit Carmen too? Ain't she fucking with your sister?"

Wow. Them stupid bitches.

"Tell me why you worse than a nigga?" She paused. "And ain't no need in your lying about it either, Crystal. Because I already knew you would fuck

Mercy before I even walked out to make the food. To be honest that's why I left. I was too embarrassed."

"First of all both of them lying." I said. "And if you thought I'd fuck her why leave out the room?"

She sighed. "Because I loved you and if the only way I could be with you was by letting you do what you wanted I figured I might as well. At least you wouldn't do it behind my back. But now I know there is nothing I can do to make you happy. You narcissistic."

I could tell in her eyes she was serious this time. And just like with Tasha she was done with me. "Look, I know I don't treat you the best—"

"Ever," she said cutting me off.

"Whatever the fuck, you know what I'm trying to say, Tiff." I wiped tears away. "I know we don't have the best relationship but it's ours and I don't want anything to happen to you tonight. If you want to argue tomorrow 'bout this then it's all good. For now it's time to leave, Tiffani." I looked out the window behind the couch to be sure Hollywood wasn't outside.

She sniffled. "And go where?"

"Get dressed," I sighed. "I'm gonna drop you over your best friend's house. But when you get there don't call your cousins or anybody else and tell them where you are." I paused. "This is important Tiffani, because I don't know what Hollywood might be willing to do." She didn't move. "Tiffani, please. I'm begging you."

She took a deep breath. "Okay." She ran around the house getting dressed and stuffing things in a red book bag. "I think it's stupid but whatever." She paused. "Where Tasha?" She asked me while dipping in and out of rooms.

"I don't know." I lied.

"Well you better catch up with her too," she continued.

"Maybe I'll look for her later." I said shaking my head. My temples throbbed so badly I thought I would pass out. "Right now I want to get you out of here."

"I got everything I'm taking," Tiff said standing in the middle of the living room. "You ready?"

"Yeah." I stood up and we walked toward the door.

"Oh when we got into that fight earlier I forgot to give you something." She stuck her hand into her pocket and pulled out a sheet of paper. "Anyway the guy Hollywood said that you or Tasha should call him to make sure her appointment went well. At first I thought he was being nice since he was taking her but now I think it's something else." She handed it to me.

After I dropped off Tiff I went to my house. The moment I was inside I grabbed a bottle of vodka, sat on the sofa and took a deep breath. After taking a large gulp I took my cell out my pocket and called Hollywood to get the status on our mother. "Hollywood," I said softly. "It's—"

"So you finally called," he said in a sly voice.

"Where the fuck is my mother?" I asked loudly. "Huh? Do you realize what I will do to your wife if something happens to my mother?" In the moment I'm so serious that I forgot Denise is already gone.

"Like I was saying, I'm glad you finally got around to calling but you can keep the threats to yourself. Before this night is over if my wife is not returned unharmed I will kill everybody you and your sister know and love. Do you understand?" He paused. "You have one hour to meet me behind that old mall with the Martin Luther King statue out front." He continued. "Bring my wife and your sister."

"But why my sister got to come?" I frowned.

"I suggest you get in the car and come now and stop asking a million questions." He said firmer. "I won't tell you again."

The moment the call was over I immediately thought about Nikki. I don't like the bitch but I know my sister loves her and if something were to happen to her she wouldn't be able to take it. Trying to quiet my breath, I sat back and attempted to remember where she lived.

But before goin' anywhere I also remembered this officer who wanted to fuck me awhile back. I ran to my bedroom, grabbed his card off the dresser and walked back into the living room. The card reads Officer Blake. On it's his cell phone number so I make the call. The phone rings once before he finally answers. "Officer Blake."

"Yes." He paused. "Who is this?"

"Officer Blake, this is Crystal Burton."

"Well, well, well," he said slyly. Like he had been waiting all his life on my call. "What did I do to deserve this surprise?"

"Actually I wanted to talk to you about something serious."

"What could be more serious than me taking you out?"

"The string of robberies in Porter Estates which I'm responsible for." I took a deep breath. "Can we talk now?"

CHAPTER TWENTY
HOLLYWOOD

*H*ollywood sat outside of Nikki's house in the backseat of a black van with no windows. Doc was driving and to the left and right of Hollywood were Cliff and Lewis his hit men. Who were ready to move on his word.

From Hollywood's viewpoint he could see Nikki getting dressed in her bedroom window. He couldn't get over how well put together she was. In a sense Nikki was a ten and the red lace underwear set she wore showcased her silky chocolate skin and in his opinion she looked good enough to eat.

I can't believe that bitch is gay. He thought to himself. "Go in and bring her to me," he told his men.

"You still want us to kill her right?" Man One questioned.

Hollywood looked at her body through the window again and took in her beauty. "Nah, bring her to me unharmed if you can." He pointed at him. "But if not, and she puts up a fight, do what you have to, to get her out that house." He rubbed his hands together. "But close the curtains before doing anything. If we can see what's going on in her room somebody else will too."

"Got it, Hollywood." Man One replied.

The van's doors opened and they quickly moved to Nikki's house to handle business, while Hollywood remained inside and thought about his wife. After everything was resolved, and she was home, he had no intention of allowing her to live in that house anymore. As a matter of fact he already purchased a beautiful home in the Buckhead area of Atlanta with enough elegance and landscape to make her feel like a queen.

From their bedroom she would be able to see a luscious green garden with the most beautiful colored flowers the mind could imagine. After this, it was definitely time for his wife to sit back, entertain close friends and family and enjoy the trap queen's lifestyle.

After about fifteen minutes of waiting on his men to return, Hollywood noticed the blinds were drawn. But where was the female? And where were his men? "What's taking them so fucking long?" He asked himself. "I know they can handle that bitch. She can't be more than a buck twenty if that."

"You want me to go check?" Doc asked.

He shook his head softly and eyed the window again. "No, but you can come with me. I'm tired of waiting around."

Before they both exited, Hollywood observed his surroundings before going inside. From what he could see there was no one looking. Feeling confident, both of them slid out of the van and crept toward the back of the house. When the coast was clear, Doc popped the lock. Once inside Hollywood felt confident that they were alone, but where was his men?

"Something ain't right, boss," Doc whispered as they both moved toward the living room. "Why don't you go wait back in the van and let me handle this." Doc removed his .9mm that was tucked in the back of his jeans. "I'll take things over from here. You don't have to worry."

"Nah, fuck that. I'm not goin' anywhere until I get that bitch," he replied as they moved further into the house. "They got my wife I want what's theirs." He paused. "Plus I need to see for myself what's going on."

As Hollywood walked further down the hallway he observed the pictures on the wall. Nikki was posed in most of them along with an older woman. Hollywood figured she was Nikki's mother and wondered where she was at the moment. Hopefully for her she wasn't in the house with her daughter.

When they finally made it to the only closed door in the hallway, Hollywood released his .45. On his signal Doc looked at him and Hollywood nodded. Doc pushed the door open a little and aimed inside. But when the door wouldn't open fully, he pushed again. It was then that they saw Cliff's body on the floor.

"Fuck is this?" Doc asked bending down. He placed his finger on Cliff's neck to check for a pulse. But his eyes were wide open so he knew he was gone.

Besides, now that they had a clearer view they could see bullet holes riddled throughout his torso and blood was everywhere. When they looked across the room they also saw Lewis's body slumped over the edge of a chair. Bullet wounds covered his neck and chest as well.

"Boss, I really think you need to leave." Doc looked at him, his gun now trembling. Could a female actually cause this much harm?

"Like I said, I'm staying," Hollywood responded. Despite the grim situation he couldn't help but smile. Even though he sent two men to take care of her, it appeared as if Nikki was able to switch the tables around. In his mind Nikki proved to be as dangerous as she was beautiful. Still, after the great violation of killing his men, Hollywood needed to get his hands on her immediately. For one he needed her as collateral to get his wife back and for two he needed her for revenge.

"Come on out, Nikki," Hollywood said. "You took two of my men but I promise you we won't be so easy."

"Yeah, I've been firing a gun since I was twelve," Doc added, looking under the bed, hoping she could hear him.

"Needless to say we're both about this shit." Hollywood looked into the closet. They went from room to room and nothing. But she wasn't a ghost so he wondered where she could be.

After thirty more seconds of searching Doc said, "I don't think she's in here."

Although Hollywood hated to admit it he said, "Me either. Fuck!" He scratched his head. "The question is where she go? We were outside in the van before we came inside. I know I didn't see her leave."

"Let me check the front of the house," Doc said.

They eased through the house some more and arrived at the kitchen. At their feet they observed a trail of blood leading toward the back door. "One of my men must've got that bitch," Hollywood said.

"Looks like it." Doc added.

Guns still aimed, both of them dipped into the backyard, on a quest to find Nikki. In the back of the house was a broken down truck but when they checked the vehicle she wasn't there either. It was as if she vanished into thin air.

"Let's go look for her on the streets," Hollywood said. "She might be on foot."

They dipped into the van and searched the city. But thirty minutes passed and still they couldn't locate her anywhere. Irritated, and defeated, Hollywood pulled out his phone and called Crystal. "I got your sister's girlfriend." He lied. "I think her name is Nikki and I'm coming for Tiffani next." He paused. "Now if you hurt my wife I will – "

"You not gonna do shit but what I say to you next," Crystal paused. "Now I'm gonna give you an address, and I expect to see you at that location. If not I'm gonna be burying your wife alive."

"Bitch, you better – "

"You got one hour!" She ended the call.

CHAPTER TWENTY-ONE
TASHA

I'm sitting in a stolen Ford outside of my house. Normally I don't steal cars but tonight I'm making an exception. Besides, I couldn't trust my ride to get me around while I searched for my mother without someone noticing it. After what Crystal told me, that Hollywood had her, I needed to make sure she was okay. Or at least try to help.

Part of me wanted to go to the cops to get their assistance but the other part knew I needed to handle this in the streets. Besides, getting them involved would bring into play all of the crimes I committed.

I was just about to go inside my crib to see who was there when I see a nigga in a black hoodie moving slowly around the back of our house. I grabbed the gun I took from Crystal and snuck behind the person before they made it to my door. My heartbeat rapidly as I rushed toward him and tackled him to the ground. Once down I turned him over to point my gun into his forehead. I'm about to blow his face off when I see it's my girl instead.

"What the…" I tucked the gun in the back of my pants. "Nikki…what the…why are you back here? What's going on?"

She moaned a little. "I've been shot, Tasha." She removed her bloody hand off the side of her stomach. "And I need help. Because I'm probably gonna die." She moaned in pain.

Her eyes closed and my heart dipped. I got off of her, lifted her up and rushed her to the stolen car. I placed her in the backseat so she could be flat. "Whatever you do, please don't die on me, baby." When I looked down at her, her eyes were still closed. "Nikki, are you hearing me, don't die on me! Now wake the fuck up because you can't be going to sleep."

She opened her eyes slowly. "Don't worry, Tasha. I won't die." Her smile was weak and melted my heart. I knew she was trying to be strong but she didn't have to. All I wanted was her to survive. "Just, please hurry and get me out of here before I...before I won't have any control."

I closed the door, ran to the driver's side and dipped behind the steering wheel before speeding away from the house. When I remembered that I was also speeding in a stolen car I took it down just a notch. "Talk to me, Nikki." I looked at her from the rearview mirror. "Nikki, talk to me so I can make sure you don't fall to sleep."

"I'm up." She moaned. "Just get me to the h...hospital." She coughed. "Please, baby. I don't feel too good."

"I'm driving as fast as I can," I paused. "But I need you to tell me something too." I looked at her through the rearview mirror. "Who, who did this to you?"

She moaned and didn't respond.

"Nikki, who did this to you?" I yelled louder.

"I don't know but it was, it was two big men." She paused. "They came into my house." Her voice got lower. "They kept telling me to come with them and I didn't, I didn't wanna go." She moaned some more. "I don't know what they wanted from me because I don't have any money."

My temples throbbed. Was this about Hollywood? It had to be! I mean, what did we think would happen when we took his wife? "And they let you get away alive?"

She giggled lightly. "Not at all. I put so…so many holes in them with my mamma's gun, they didn't know what happened." She paused. "But one of them got me too."

I loved my bitch even more. Hearing how she defended herself was so her. Guns were her life and I'm sure they had no clue who they was fucking with. "But how you get away?"

"Went to my neighbor's backyard and hid in their shed. OUCH!" She screamed. "I knew, I knew they wouldn't think to go next door so I figured I would be safe. Plus my blood trail got lost in the grass." She paused. "What do you think they wanted, Tasha?"

I knew it was Hollywood and I felt bad for getting her involved in all of this shit. And to be honest it was making me hate Crystal even more. As if I needed any other reasons. "Don't worry about all that right now, Nikki. As a matter of fact I don't want you to talk too much."

"You gonna marry me after this shit, Tasha?" She asked. "Because something tells me this was somehow related to you. So the least you could do is be my Hersband." She paused. "And the baby...I'm worried about the..."

"The baby will be fine," I said remembering she was pregnant. "The baby will be just fine."

"I...I hope so," she said softly. "We gonna have more than one baby?" She said in a low voice. "'Cause I always wanted a huge family."

I continued to steer the car. "You make it out of this and we can have as many kids as you want, Nikki."

"You promise?" She moaned louder.

LEVEL UP

"I promise. I put that on everything."

When my cell phone rung I answered even though the number was blocked. "Who this?" I continued steering with one hand.

"It's me, Crystal. Look, Tasha, I know you said you don't wanna hear from me but I gotta tell you something."

I immediately hung up and threw the phone into the passenger seat. When she continued to call I wondered if she had any more info on ma so I answered again. "What the fuck you want, Crystal? Whatever it is, make it quick. I don't have any time."

"I wanted to tell you, that I'm so sorry," she paused. "I keep thinking about how close we were a week ago and how far apart we are now. And I don't like this for us. We sisters. And I know you always forgive and I know I always fuck up but I need to know if you can forgive me just one more time. I don't want anything from you, sis. Just your forgiveness."

Just hearing her voice caused my temples to throb, especially with my bitch doing badly in the back seat. So forgiving her was the last thing on my mind. "You got ma or not?"

"No...I'm trying to—"

"If you don't got ma there ain't no way I could ever forgive you so don't even ask."

I thought about telling her that I have Nikki and that if she died it would also be her fault but I don't bother. It ain't worth it for me. Crystal ain't worth it for me. Instead I end the call, tossed it on the passenger seat and continue down the road.

When I heard a sound from my girl like she's taking her last breath I panicked and the car swerved. "Nikki...Nikki! Answer me! Answer me please!"

CHAPTER TWENTY-TWO
CRYSTAL

When I pulled Denise's car up behind the building and saw a black van and some huge man standing outside of it, I thought about turning around and running. Instead I talk myself off the ledge. *Crystal, you started this drama and now you have to finish it. If you turn back all he's gonna do is go after your sister.*

Nah, I couldn't do that. It was time to push forward. I had tried to reach Tasha to let her know Hollywood was possibly coming to kill her girlfriend but she didn't want to talk. I understood though. I wouldn't want to talk to me either.

I still took care of business. I made sure Tiffani was safe and I confessed to all the robberies with the cop in the event something happened to me tonight. I really wanted my sister to be able to live her dreams and go on with her life. I just hope my plans work.

After clearing up my loose ends I went to the area but where was Hollywood?

Tasha's right about me though. From the beginning I was fucking up and always causing her problems where there shouldn't have been any. It was time for me to answer to everything. So I pulled up beside the van, parked and hopped out. The moment my car door closed two large men rushed over to me and ran their hands over my body. I guess checking for weapons.

"What's going on?" I asked looking around from where I stood. "And where is Hollywood?"

"Shut the fuck up, bitch," the large man said. "We asking the questions around here." When they were done touching my ass and tits, one of them turned around and yelled, "She's clean."

The huge man opened the back door leading to the van and Hollywood eased out as if he had no worries. He cracked his knuckles and approached me slowly. I thought he was about to hit me, or even shoot me but for now he doesn't.

I took a deep breath. Instead of being intimidated I said real calmly, "Where's my mother?"

He smiled. "Where is your sister?"

"She ain't here."

He nodded. "Who would have thought, as pretty as you are, that you could be so much trouble?" He stepped closer. "But let's do one thing at a time." He looked me over from the top of my head to my feet. "You know what as much shit as you talk, you probably should've been a man. I mean think about it. You fuck bitches and everything." He paused. "Instead you ain't nothing but a little bitch who's way out of her fucking league."

I smirked. "Big things come in sexy packages." I paused. "At least that's what I always hear."

He laughed. "Is that right?"

I continued to smile until it wiped away from my face slowly. "Where the fuck is my mother, Hollywood?"

He crossed his arms over his chest and sucked his teeth. "I don't know. Where do you think she is? For all I know she could be looking down on you right now." He looked up at the sky. "That is, if that's the kind of thing you believe in. Angels and all."

My heart rate increased. I knew immediately what he was about to say before he even said it. Even if Hollywood lied and said she was alive, I could now feel that's no longer the case. She's gone off this earth. I thought about that dream I had awhile back. There was a house and when I walked inside of it ma was there with some of my other family members who died. Tasha was there too, but she was on the outside of the house which meant she was still alive.

"Nah, let me stop playing. Your mother's okay," he said. "And once I get my wife I'll take you to her. Now, where is my wife, Crystal? Time is ticking and my patience is running thin."

I swallowed and looked up at him. Slowly my lips parted and I said, "Your whore is dead." The moment I uttered the words I felt light. Like I made a huge mistake I couldn't take back.

"Fuck you mean dead, bitch?" He roared and clenched his fist tightly. "Did you really come out here just to be suicidal?"

I laughed. "I don't know what you want me to say to be honest." I shrugged. "I mean, is there any other language for dead? She gone. Like eliminated and you'll never see her again. Maybe that's clear enough for you."

Hollywood looked at his men and I could see him trembling like he was about to explode. "Go check the car, Doc," he said to the large man.

This was the moment I knew would come when I decided to meet Hollywood. It would definitely mean the end. Quickly the large men walked to the car and searched inside. Looking back at Hollywood he yelled, "She ain't here!"

He looked at me sternly. "Where is my fuckin' wife, Crystal? I'm not playing games anymore."

"She's inside the car," I smiled and looked behind me. "All you gotta do is check the trunk." His man popped the trunk.

Hollywood's eyes widened but he stayed in front of me. As if preventing me from trying to get away. But where was I going to go? "If my wife is in that trunk you gonna die. Do you hear—"

"She's in here!" The man yelled. "It's…I'm, I'm sorry, Hollywood," He stuttered.

Hollywood walked away and up to the man. I turned around to look at them both. "Is…is she alive, Doc?"

"No." He backed away and covered his mouth. "She gone."

Hollywood glared at me and walked back over to me quickly. "You come to me with my wife in the trunk of her car?" He slapped me down. I stayed there. "Do you actually think you gonna live?" He paused. "Do you know what kind of woman she was? What kind of person you fucking killed?" He grabbed my throat and squeezed. I could barely breathe. "You think I'm a fucking joke?"

I clawed at his hands but was able to say, "Who said I wanted to live?" He released me and I rubbed my neck, before falling to the ground. "Just so you know my sister ain't have nothing to do with this. Your wife had been getting on my nerves since the moment I picked that bitch up from your house. So I got rid of her. And you should also know she fought to the death. But eventually I took her out anyway."

He walked up to me and looked down. "A quick death is too easy for this bitch." He looked at Doc. "Torture her ass until you get tired. And then I want so many holes in her I can see through her body."

I heard the click of many guns before I was lifted up and moved toward the van. When I looked up at the sky I thought about my sister and how much I want her to succeed. "I hope you can forgive me now, Tasha. Goodbye."

CHAPTER TWENTY-THREE

TASHA

(TWO YEARS LATER)

I was sitting on my bed looking at a picture of my mother and sister at our party. I was trying to remember a time when things were good but couldn't. Too much pain. Since I was born there always seemed to be some dark presence over our family but it didn't mean I didn't love them.

Ever since we buried her and my sister two years ago today, I felt lost. Plus so much went down in this short time. After the trial where Hollywood and his men went to jail for their murder Nikki and I moved to Houston where we could raise our son. It turned out Nikki was able to sustain the pregnancy despite getting shot. It amazed me how strong she was.

We couldn't wait to leave Adamsville and everything behind. Including furniture and our clothes. Tiffani kept in contact with us from time to time but after awhile it seemed weird talking to her about old times. Besides, the last thing I heard was that she was on drugs and I didn't think it would be a good idea to have her in our lives.

"It's time to go to bed, Lil' Chris." I named my son after my sister. He was called Christal. When he was under the sheets I pulled the sheet over his head. "We goin' to the park tomorrow and I'm gonna buy you some candy and everything." He cheesed a little but didn't understand everything I was saying. "I love you very much."

I stood up and moved toward the door. "Night, night," he said.

I winked at him and walked out his room. The moment I closed the door I saw Nikki sitting in the living room reading a book. She was still as sexy as ever except now she was my wife.

But instead of sitting with her I walked into the bathroom, closed the door and slid to the floor. I could smell the scent of bleach from the toilet that Nikki cleaned earlier and smiled. Since we moved together there wasn't any time I could remember that she didn't prepare a hot meal and keep a clean house. She was amazing to live with but sometimes I feel trapped. It's almost as if I need my own space. Or maybe I missed the robbery lifestyle I had become accustomed to.

Feeling frustrated, I looked up at the ceiling. When my sister died I replayed in my mind how our last call ended. I couldn't stop thinking about when our lives changed the day Hollywood walked into the post office. But more than anything I couldn't forget how I treated her when she begged for forgiveness.

"Crystal, it's me again. I know you up there doing everything possible to get on God's nerves." I laughed. "And I know you're looking over me and my son too." I looked down at my hands. "He's a cool kid ain't he?" A tear rolled down my face and I wiped it away. "I just wanted to tell you that I'm sorry for not being there when you needed me the last time we spoke. I want you to know that I'm gonna love my son like I did you when we were young. And that I will never abandon him no matter how hard things get. Ever." I shook my head. "I miss you, Crystal. Tell ma I miss her too. I'll see you soon."

I stood up, wiped the back of my pants and walked into the living room. Once there I sat on the sofa next to Nikki and she immediately laid her head into my lap as I stroke her hair. It was crazy to think about the history.

After getting shot, Nikki lost a lot of blood and almost didn't make it. The crazy part was we shared the same blood type and I told them to drain me until I died if it meant saving her life. Luckily they didn't need to do that but things looked bad for a long time. She took a bullet to the ribs but still survived.

"The Chinese food was bad?" She asked looking up at me. "Even if it wasn't I definitely have had better."

"Nah, it wasn't the food." I sighed. "Why you say that?"

"Because you were in the bathroom for a long time." She paused. "What were you doing, talking to your sister again?"

I sighed. "Yeah, but I'm cool now." I rubbed her warm cheek.

"Crystal did what she did because she wanted you to be happy. And I know you so I know you are getting bored living the drama free lifestyle. All I ask is that you give us a chance and see how it feels."

I smiled. "What if I can't get rid of the feeling?"

She shrugged. "We can talk about that when we get there. I mean, I know you a hood bitch from Adamsville but this is our new life. And I want the happily ever after." She paused. "Please?"

"I guess I gotta be good with it then." I bent down and kissed her lips. *For now.* I thought.

By NIKKI. K

The Cartel Publications Order Form

www.thecartelpublications.com

Inmates **ONLY** receive novels for $10.00 per book.
(Mail Order **MUST** come from inmate directly to receive discount)

Shyt List 1	_____	$15.00
Shyt List 2	_____	$15.00
Shyt List 3	_____	$15.00
Shyt List 4	_____	$15.00
Shyt List 5	_____	$15.00
Pitbulls In A Skirt	_____	$15.00
Pitbulls In A Skirt 2	_____	$15.00
Pitbulls In A Skirt 3	_____	$15.00
Pitbulls In A Skirt 4	_____	$15.00
Pitbulls In A Skirt 5	_____	$15.00
Victoria's Secret	_____	$15.00
Poison 1	_____	$15.00
Poison 2	_____	$15.00
Hell Razor Honeys	_____	$15.00
Hell Razor Honeys 2	_____	$15.00
A Hustler's Son	_____	$15.00
A Hustler's Son 2	_____	$15.00
Black and Ugly	_____	$15.00
Black and Ugly As Ever	_____	$15.00
Year Of The Crackmom	_____	$15.00
Deadheads	_____	$15.00
The Face That Launched A Thousand Bullets	_____	$15.00
The Unusual Suspects	_____	$15.00
Miss Wayne & The Queens of DC	_____	$15.00
LaFamilia Divided	_____	$15.00
Raunchy	_____	$15.00
Raunchy 2	_____	$15.00
Raunchy 3	_____	$15.00
Mad Maxxx	_____	$15.00
Quita's Dayscare Center	_____	$15.00
Quita's Dayscare Center 2	_____	$15.00
Pretty Kings	_____	$15.00
Pretty Kings 2	_____	$15.00
Pretty Kings 3	_____	$15.00
Pretty Kings 4	_____	$15.00
Silence Of The Nine	_____	$15.00
Silence Of The Nine 2	_____	$15.00
Silence Of The Nine 3	_____	$15.00
Prison Throne	_____	$15.00
Drunk & Hot Girls	_____	$15.00
Hersband Material	_____	$15.00
The End: How To Write A Bestselling Novel In 30 Days (Non-Fiction Guide)	_____	$15.00
Upscale Kittens	_____	$15.00
Wake & Bake Boys	_____	$15.00
Young & Dumb	_____	$15.00
Young & Dumb 2:	_____	$15.00
Tranny 911	_____	$15.00
Tranny 911: Dixie's Rise	_____	$15.00

LEVEL UP

First Comes Love, Then Comes Murder _____	$15.00
Luxury Tax _____	$15.00
The Lying King _____	$15.00
Crazy Kind Of Love _____	$15.00
And They Call Me God _____	$15.00
The Ungrateful Bastards _____	$15.00
Lipstick Dom _____	$15.00
A School of Dolls _____	$15.00
Hoetic Justice _____	$15.00
Goon _____	$15.00
KALI: Raunchy Relived _____	$15.00
Skeezers _____	$15.00
You Kissed Me, Now I Own You _____	$15.00
Nefarious _____	$15.00
Redbone 3: The Rise of The Fold _____	$15.00
The Fold _____	$15.00
Clown Niggas _____	$15.00
The One You Shouldn't Trust _____	$15.00
The WHORE The Wind Blew My Way _____	$15.00
She Brings The Worst Kind _____	$15.00
The House That Crack Built _____	$15.00
The House That Crack Built 2 _____	$15.00
The House That Crack Built 3 _____	$15.00
Level Up _____	$15.00

(**Redbone 1** & **2** are **NOT** Cartel Publications novels and if **ordered** the cost is **FULL** price of $15.00 **each**. **No Exceptions**.)

Please add $5.00 **PER BOOK** for shipping and handling.

The Cartel Publications * P.O. BOX 486 OWINGS MILLS MD 21117

Name: _____

Address: _____

City/State: _____

Contact/Email: _____

Please allow 7-10 **BUSINESS** days *before* shipping.

The Cartel Publications is **NOT** responsible for **Prison Orders** rejected!

NO RETURNS and NO REFUNDS.

NO PERSONAL CHECKS ACCEPTED

STAMPS NO LONGER ACCEPTED

By NIKKI. K